Jack Higgins lived in Belfast till the age of twelve. Leaving school at fifteen, he spent three years with the Royal Horse Guards, serving on the East German border during the Cold War. His subsequent employment included occupations as diverse as circus roustabout, truck driver, clerk and, after taking an honours degree in sociology and social psychology, teacher and university lecturer.

The Eagle Has Landed turned him into an international bestselling author, and his novels have since sold over 250 million copies and have been translated into fifty-five languages. Many of them have also been made into successful films. His recent bestselling novels include *Bad Company*, *A Fine Night for Dying*, *Dark Justice*, *The Killing Ground*, *Rough Justice*, *A Darker Place* and *The Wolf at the Door*.

In 1995 Jack Higgins was awarded an honorary doctorate by Leeds Metropolitan University. He is a fellow of the Royal Society of Arts and an expert scuba diver and marksman. He lives on Jersey.

ALSO BY JACK HIGGINS

JACK HIGGINS

CRY OF
THE HUNTER

HARPER

Harper
An imprint of HarperCollins*Publishers*
77–85 Fulham Palace Road,
Hammersmith, London W6 8JB

www.harpercollins.co.uk

This paperback edition 2010
1

First published in Great Britain by John Long Ltd 1960
Arrow Edition 1979
Penguin Books Edition 1998

Copyright © Harry Patterson 1960

Jack Higgins asserts the moral right to
be identified as the author of this work

A catalogue record for this book is
available from the British Library

ISBN: 978-0-00-723489-9

Typeset in Sabon by Palimpsest Book Production Limited,
Grangemouth, Stirlingshire

Printed and bound in Great Britain by
Clays Ltd, St Ives plc

PUBLISHER'S NOTE

Cry Of The Hunter was first published in the UK by John Long in 1960 and later by *Arrow* in 1979. It was originally published under the name of Harry Patterson, an author who later became known to millions as Jack Higgins.

This amazing novel has been out of print for some years, and in 2010, it seemed to the author and his publishers that it was a pity to leave such a good story languishing on his shelves. So we are delighted to be able to bring back *Cry Of The Hunter* for the pleasure of the vast majority of us who never had a chance to read the earlier editions.

For Uncle David

1

Fallon awakened suddenly and completely and lay staring blindly into the darkness. Gradually the room began to take shape as his eyes became accustomed to the gloom, and he reached for cigarettes to the small table that stood beside the bed. He closed his eyes against the sudden flare of the match and inhaled deeply. His throat was dry and his mouth tasted bad. He groaned and his searching hand groped again in the darkness until it located a bottle.

He pulled the cork with his teeth and swallowed deeply. The whisky burned its way down to his stomach, filling him with a nausea that was followed by a pleasant glow.

He leaned back against the pillows with a sigh of relief.

Rain spattered on the window with ghostly fingers and he looked at the luminous dial of his watch and saw that it was eleven-thirty. He wondered what day it was. He lifted the bottle to his lips again and considered the point. He was still dressed so he must have been drunk when he went to bed. That much was obvious, but beyond that point it was difficult to go for memory had a way of playing tricks on him. He decided he must be getting old and took another generous swallow from the bottle. He remembered getting up and it had been a fine morning. He had tried to work but the words had refused to come and the whisky hadn't helped. It hadn't helped at all. One thing was certain. He couldn't have lain there for more than a day because his watch was still going.

A sudden gust of wind loosed a tendril of ivy from the wall and set it tapping against the window with an eerie monotony that was unnerving. He shivered and raised the bottle to his lips again. It was empty and he dropped it carelessly to the floor and decided to get up.

He stubbed his cigarette into the ashtray that stood on the small table and then, suddenly, he was alone with the darkness and it moved in on him, pushing against his body with a terrible weightless pressure that was terrifying in its relentless force. The darkness moved in and moved out and a curious sibilant whisper rippled through the void. For a moment he swayed on the edge of panic and then he hurled aside the bedclothes and lurched to his feet.

His trembling fingers fumbled with matches and a small flame blossomed out of the darkness. He turned up the wick of the bedside lamp with his free hand and touched it with the match. Light spread to each corner of the room, driving the shadows before it, and he sat down on the bed and lit another cigarette with hands that shook slightly.

After a while he took the lamp and went into the bathroom. His shirt was damp with perspiration and he stripped it from his body and sluiced his head and shoulders with cold water. As he dried himself he examined his face in the mirror. Dark, sombre eyes that were too deeply set in their sockets, stared out at him with an expression he could no longer analyse even to himself. The ugly, puckered scar that slanted across his right cheek, lifted the corner of his mouth giving him an oddly bitter and sardonic expression that was accentuated by the dark fringe of his beard.

He returned to the bedroom and rummaged in a drawer until he found a clean shirt. He pulled it quickly over his head and buttoned it with fingers that had found their sureness again and then he took the lamp and left the room. It was cold in the stone-flagged passage and he passed quickly into the kitchen. He took a bundle of kindling from a box in one corner and went into the main room of the cottage.

His typewriter rested on a table by the window and the floor was littered with crumpled balls of paper. He gathered them together quickly and used them to start the fire with. In a few moments the dry kindling was burning brightly and he carefully added logs from the pile in the hearth.

He sat back on his heels and stared deeply into the bright flames and after a while, when the fire was burning steadily, he straightened up and moved to a dresser on the far side of the room. He took down a fresh bottle of whisky, turned down the lamp, and sat in a chair by the fire, a glass in one hand and the bottle on the floor beside him.

The flames flickered across the oak-beamed ceiling, casting fantastic shadows that writhed and twisted constantly. The liquor in the glass gleamed, amber and gold, and Fallon savoured it slowly and felt its warmth flowing into him. He sighed with pleasure and started to refill his glass and suddenly a light flashed through the window, illuminating the far wall for a second, and disappearing as quickly as it had come.

He moved quickly to the window and peered out into the darkness and the driving rain. There was nothing to be seen. He was about to turn away when car headlights appeared from a dip in the road below. The car was moving slowly and then it appeared to stop. He watched it for a few moments until the lights moved forward again and turned into the track that led to the cottage.

Fallon pushed the typewriter out of the way and opened a drawer in the table. He took out a Luger automatic pistol and an electric torch. He checked the action of the Luger and then opened the door and moved out into the covered porch.

The car came to a halt a few feet away and the engine was turned off. For a little while there was silence and he waited patiently in the darkness as the rain hammered steadily into the ground. He heard one of the doors open and there was a snatch of conversation and then the door closed again and two figures came towards him. They paused a few feet away from the porch and a voice said, 'It's a God-forsaken spot. Do you think he's here?'

Fallon eased the safety-catch off and held the Luger against his right thigh. He raised the torch and said quietly, 'He's here!' Light stabbed through the darkness, picking out the start-led faces of the two men who stood before him.

There was silence and then a voice that he had not heard for many years said, 'Is it your-self, Martin?'

For a moment he held the torch steady on them and then he directed the beam down-wards and said, 'You'd better come in. Watch the step with that leg of yours, O'Hara.'

He went back into the cottage and turned up the lamp. The two visitors followed him in and closed the door behind them. Fallon turned and faced them. He suddenly realized that he was still holding the Luger in one hand and he laughed shortly and put it down. The younger of the two men said, 'Old habits die hard.'

Fallon shrugged. 'What would you be knowing about my old habits?'

The man he had addressed as O'Hara laughed. 'A good answer,' he said. 'A good answer.' He was old with sagging shoulders and he supported his massive frame on a stick.

'You'd better take your coat off and sit

down,' Fallon told him. He turned away and took two extra glasses from a shelf.

The younger man helped O'Hara off with his coat and the old man sat down in a chair by the fire with a sigh of relief. 'Ah, now, is it a drop of the right stuff you're going to offer us?' he said as Fallon came forward with the glasses.

Fallon poured a generous measure into a glass and gave it to him. 'Who's your friend?' he said.

O'Hara laughed again. 'Fancy me forgetting my manners like that. This is Jimmy Doolan. He's wanted to meet you for a long time, Martin.'

Doolan smiled quietly and held out his hand He was a small, quiet man with good capable hands and a Dublin accent. 'I've dreamed of this day, Mr Fallon. You've been a hero to me since I was a kid.'

Fallon grunted. 'A fine sort of hero.' He handed Doolan a glass of whisky. 'A lot of bloody good it did me.'

A puzzled expression appeared on Doolan's face and O'Hara leaned forward and said easily, 'Now then, Martin. Don't tell me you've turned bitter in your old age.'

Fallon shrugged and sat down. 'Bitter? It depends how you look at it. It's one of the few luxuries I can afford these days.'

There was another short, uneasy pause before O'Hara said, 'How's the writing going? I never seem to see anything under your name.'

Fallon nodded. 'You never will. I write thrillers under two different names. They wouldn't interest you. They don't even interest me. All they do successfully is pay the bills and keep me in whisky.'

Doolan leaned forward. 'Don't you ever feel like doing something else, Mr Fallon?'

Fallon looked at him for a moment and then smiled. 'Not particularly. What would you suggest?'

Doolan fumbled for words. 'Well, now, what you were doing before was not such a bad thing.'

'I was in prison before,' Fallon told him. 'I was doing hard labour. Would you have me do that again?' There was a short, tense silence and he stood up and said, 'What is it, O'Hara? What do you want with me?'

O'Hara sighed heavily and poked a log that was threatening to fall into the hearth, back into place with the end of his walking stick. 'The Organization needs you, Martin,' he said. 'It needs you bad.'

Fallon started so that whisky slopped over the edge of his glass. He gazed at O'Hara in astonishment and then he laughed harshly. 'The Organization needs me?' he said and there was incredulity in his voice. 'After all these years it needs me?'

O'Hara nodded slowly. 'It's right enough. Doolan and I have been asked to come and see you.'

Fallon began to laugh uncontrollably. 'That's rich,' he said. 'That's damned rich.'

Doolan jumped up and said angrily, 'What's so funny, Mr Fallon?'

'The fact that the Organization can bloody well do without me,' Fallon said. 'That's what's so funny.'

Doolan swore savagely and turned to O'Hara. 'Is this the great Martin Fallon?

Swilling his guts with whisky and rotting in a back-country pigsty?'

Fallon moved so quickly that Doolan didn't stand a chance. A fist caught him high on the right cheek and he stumbled, tripped over a loose rug and fell heavily to the floor. Fallon hauled him to his feet and pushed him down into a chair. 'Listen to me,' he said, and his voice was ice-cold. 'When I was a schoolboy I lived and breathed the I.R.A. I joined when I was seventeen. When I was twenty-two I was the leader of the Organization in Ulster. I was a name in the land. I'm forty years of age and I've spent nine of them in prison. I've done my share for Ireland.'

'Now then, Martin,' O'Hara said soothingly. 'No one is denying what you've suffered but it should only strengthen your resolve to fight until the whole of Ireland is free again.'

Fallon threw back his head and laughed savagely. 'For God's sake, are you still handing out that kind of clap-trap? The country is as free as it wants to be. If they ever want to change things north of the border they'll do it through the government and through law. Guns and bombs will only serve to make them realize how well off they are without us.'

Doolan groaned and shook his head several times and Fallon handed him a glass of whisky which the small man swallowed at a gulp. After a while he fingered his face gingerly and said with a wry smile. 'That's a hell of a wallop you've got, Mr Fallon, and no mistake.'

Fallon grinned and sat down. 'I'm sorry I lost my temper,' he said, 'but you touched me on a raw spot.'

'It's a thing I wouldn't advise any man to do,' Doolan said feelingly.

O'Hara coughed and spat into the fire. 'We wouldn't have come to you if there was anyone else, Martin. It's desperate work and you're the only man for it, and that's a fact.'

'You're wasting your time,' Fallon told him.

Doolan moved uneasily and there was puzzlement in his voice. 'Do you mean to tell me you won't help us, Mr Fallon?'

Fallon took out a cigarette and lit it. 'That's

about the size of it.' Doolan turned helplessly to O'Hara and Fallon went on. 'That old spider there knew damned well that I wouldn't stir a finger. He'd no right to bring you here.'

O'Hara raised his eyes piously to the ceiling and Doolan said, 'But why now? You were the greatest of them all. You were worshipped throughout the length and breadth of Ireland.'

Fallon nodded and said lightly, 'If only I'd got myself killed. It would have been even better. Another martyr to the cause.' Doolan made a sudden exclamation of disgust and turned away and Fallon said seriously, 'How old are you, lad? How many times have you been over the border? I've spent more than a lifetime over there. I've spent eternity many times over. I've been chased throughout the length and breadth of Ulster, and England, too. Five years ago I escaped from Dartmoor Prison. For three weeks I was hunted like an animal before I reached this country again. Oh, I was the great hero until I told them at Headquarters that I was through. O'Hara was there. He knows what happened.'

'You were a sick man, Martin,' O'Hara said smoothly. 'You weren't in your right mind.'

Fallon laughed grimly. 'I was right in my mind for the first time in my life,' he said. 'I'd had plenty of time to think it over.'

'But you can't leave the Organization,' Doolan said. 'Once you're a member, it's for life. There's only one way out.'

'I know,' Fallon said. 'Feet first, but that's where I had them, you see. You can't court-martial and shoot the greatest living hero you've got. That wouldn't do at all because the rot might set in. People might begin to think there was something wrong. No, you just put up with him and heave a sigh of relief when he buries himself in the wilds. And who knows – if you're really lucky he might even drink himself into the grave.'

Doolan stared helplessly at him and O'Hara said, calmly, 'What a one for the words you always were, Martin. What a one. But we still haven't got down to business.'

Fallon shook his head and, despite himself, a reluctant smile came to his lips. 'You're wasting your time, O'Hara,' he said. 'I'm safe here. Four strong walls and a roof to keep out the rain, my typewriter to pay the bills and plenty of booze.'

'Just so,' the old man replied. 'The whisky to try and fill the emptiness in you.' He cackled suddenly. 'Why man, the Irish Sea itself couldn't fill that hole inside you.'

For a brief moment Fallon's face slipped and a terrible expression came into his eyes and then he regained control and smiled lightly.

'It's you that should be writing the books and not me,' he said.

O'Hara leaned back, a satisfied smile on his face. 'Are you ready to hear why we've come, then?'

For a moment Fallon hesitated and then curiosity got the better of him. He shrugged. 'All right. I'm listening. It can't do any harm.'

O'Hara nodded and Doolan leaned forward and lowered his voice. 'Have you heard of Patrick Rogan, Mr Fallon?'

Fallon frowned. 'I knew him well. A mad, hair-brained fanatic. He was shot dead in a running fight with the police on the Belfast Docks.'

'He had a son,' O'Hara said, quietly.

'Yes, he had a son,' Fallon said. 'Shamus they called him. He was killed in nineteen-forty-five in a raid on a police barracks in County Down. I've forgotten the name of the place.'

'There was another son,' Doolan said. 'Did you know that? Only a nipper when his father was killed. Don't you read the papers here, Mr Fallon?'

'I'm careful not to,' Fallon said.

Doolan smiled briefly and went on. 'Two years ago there was a clean sweep made in Belfast and the polis lifted most of the leaders. Patrick Rogan was only twenty and he hadn't been over there long but he rose to the occasion and proved himself his father's son. He took over leadership of the Organization and was so successful we left him in charge.'

Fallon raised his eyebrows. 'He must be quite a boy.'

'He is indeed, Mr Fallon,' Doolan said, 'and one we can't do without. He's walked

the path of danger these two years, a hero
and a legend to his people.' He paused and
the only sound in the room was the crackling of the logs in the fire and the drumming
of the rain against the window. O'Hara
coughed asthmatically and Doolan said,
heavily, 'He was taken the day before
yesterday.'

There was another short silence and then
Fallon said, 'Well, it comes to us all in the
end. He lost, that's all.'

'We must have him out,' O'Hara said
suddenly. 'He must never stand trial.'

Fallon's eyes narrowed and he looked first
at Doolan, who dropped his gaze, and then at
O'Hara. He laughed briefly. 'What kind of a
line are you trying to give me? Why shouldn't
he stand trial? I stood trial. What makes
Rogan so different?'

Doolan sighed and said to O'Hara, 'We'll
have to tell him the truth. It's no good.'

O'Hara nodded. 'I knew we would. I didn't
think he'd be fooled for a minute.'

Doolan turned to Fallon. He seemed to
search for words and then he said, 'You see,

Mr Fallon, Rogan is everything I said he was. He's served his country well. He's done good work in Ulster, but . . .'

'He's not to be trusted,' O'Hara said. 'It could be the end of the Organization in Ulster if he ever stands trial.'

Fallon poured himself another drink and said coolly, 'The work of years going up in smoke, eh? That wouldn't be so good. How can he do it?'

Doolan sighed wearily and leaned back in his chair. 'The polis are holding him at Castlemore. He managed to get a message smuggled out to us yesterday. He says we must get him out before they move him to Belfast. If we leave him to stand trial he swears he'll make a deal with the polis. He'll tell them everything they want to know about the Organization in Ulster if they promise to go easy on him.'

Fallon frowned. 'He must be mad. He knows the first thing he'd get from the Organization, even if he was freed, would be a bullet. He'd do better to take his sentence and bide his time.'

O'Hara shook his head. 'There'll be no

biding his time, Martin, if he is sentenced. He shot a peeler dead and crippled another. They'll hang him so high the crows won't be able to get at him.'

Fallon whistled softly. 'God help him then. They're hard men to deal with at the best of times. Devils, when one of their own has been killed.'

'You can see why we came to you, Mr Fallon,' Doolan said. 'There's nobody else left up there. Nobody that's good enough to handle a job like this.'

Fallon laughed coldly. 'And you think I'm going to stick my head into that hornets' nest? You must be mad.'

'You mean you refuse to help us?' Doolan said.

'I wouldn't raise a finger,' Fallon told him. 'Rogan shot a peeler. He knew what he was doing. Now he can take the consequences.' There was a hard finality in his tone.

Doolan turned to O'Hara, but the old man didn't seem to be attending. He sat erect, his head slightly on one side as if he was listening for something. Suddenly he pulled himself to his feet and went across to the window. He peered out and when he turned there was a slight smile on his face. 'Don't worry, Jimmy,' he said. 'It's going to be all right. The trouble with you is you don't understand the Irish temperament.' He chuckled to himself and shuffled back to his chair by the fire.

At that moment Fallon became aware of the sound of a car engine muffled by the rain. He turned and said, 'What dirty trick have you got up your sleeve now, O'Hara?'

The old man smiled genially and took out his pipe. 'No tricks, Martin. Psychology. It's a grand thing, and after all – we must move with the times.'

As the car stopped outside Fallon filled his glass with a steady hand and poured the whisky down his throat in one easy swallow. He said, 'You're wasting your time, old spider.'

A knock sounded on the door and Doolan stood up, a frown on his face, and said to O'Hara, 'What's going on? You told me nothing of this?'

O'Hara smiled. 'A small plan of my own.'

He nodded reassuringly. 'Answer the door, Jimmy.'

Doolan walked slowly to the door and opened it. At first Fallon saw only the man and then he realized that a woman was leaning on his arm. For a moment he thought that she was wearing a cloak and then, as she moved forward into the light, he saw that she had an old, yellowing trenchcoat thrown lightly over her shoulders. In one hand she held a cane with which she tentatively felt her way. Her hair was snow-white and shone like a halo in the lamplight.

A terrible unease touched Fallon's heart and his hand tightened around his glass. The woman halted in the centre of the room and her escort moved back to the door. O'Hara got to his feet and said, 'I'm glad you could come, Maureen.' He moved forward and took her hand. 'This must seem like a strange meeting to you, but I knew you would want to speak with him before he goes to save Patrick.'

The woman turned her face into the light and stared across the room with opaque, sightless eyes. 'Where are you, Martin Fallon?' she said.

O'Hara turned to Fallon, his face expressionless. 'Martin, this is Patrick Rogan's mother come to see you.'

Fallon placed his glass carefully on the floor and got to his feet. When he looked at O'Hara there was contempt on his face and the old man dropped his eyes. He moved forward and said, 'I'm here, Mrs Rogan.'

She raised her hand and gently touched his face with the tips of her fingers. The skin was drawn tightly over her bones and it was parchment yellow. She looked incredibly ancient and timeless and there was the mark of great suffering upon her face. She said, 'I've given a husband and a son to the cause, Martin Fallon. I've given enough.'

He took her hand gently in his. 'Enough and to spare, Mrs Rogan.'

'You will save Patrick for me,' she said. 'You will bring him home safely.' It was a statement of fact that admitted no denial.

Fallon looked into the vacant, useless eyes and tried to find words to answer her. Bitterness welled up inside him and a deep hatred for O'Hara who had placed him in such an impossible situation. How could he say no and continue to look upon the suffering in the face before him? He tried to speak and then, as if she sensed the turmoil within him, an expression of panic crossed her face and her hand tightened on his. It was as if she could see into the very depths of his soul. She swayed suddenly and he reached forward to steady her. 'You will save him?' she said in anguish. 'You must!'

There was a great silence as she waited for his answer and Fallon smiled and gently squeezed her hand. 'I'll bring him safe home to you, Mrs Rogan,' he said. In his heart he knew that from the moment she entered the room, fate had taken control.

She sighed as though from a great distance, and swayed again and he steadied her and said, 'You'd better come and lie down for a while.'

She nodded several times and leaned heavily on his arm. Doolan moved quickly to open the door for them and they went out into the passage and passed through into the bedroom.

* * *

When Fallon returned O'Hara and Doolan were in the middle of a heated argument. Doolan said, 'I still think it was a shameful trick, using the woman.'

O'Hara raised a hand. 'Don't talk to me of tricks,' he said. 'In this game anything goes. Ask that man there,' he added, pointing to Fallon as he joined them. 'He's used a few in his time.'

Fallon threw himself down into his chair. 'Oh, he's right enough,' he said to Doolan. 'Anything goes. It's the only way to get things done, but the old spider's over-reached himself this time.'

'And how do you make that out?' O'Hara demanded.

'Simple – the whole thing's doomed to failure from the very beginning. Do you think for a moment that the police have the slightest intention of letting anyone even get near to Rogan? There are three thousand peelers over there who want one thing very badly at the moment. They want to see Patrick Rogan hang and they'll make damned sure nobody interferes.'

O'Hara nodded and said calmly, 'I know that. I told you it was a desperate business, but if anyone can do it, you can.' Fallon gave an exclamation of disgust and the old man went on. 'No, Martin, I mean it. The trouble with most of the boys when they get over the border is that they begin to crack right way. They take the whole business too damned seriously. Now, you never did.'

'Are you mad?' Doolan said indignantly. 'I've never heard such nonsense in my life.'

Fallon threw back his head and laughed. 'He's right though,' he said. 'I never did.' He glanced at Doolan's outraged face and sobered up. 'The only way to survive over there is to treat the whole thing like a game,' he said. 'It's like war – it is war. But it isn't like the books or the ballads at all. It's dirty and dangerous and incredibly stupid.'

'And that's the only philosophy that can ever achieve the impossible,' O'Hara said.

Fallon leaned forward. 'You'd better give me what information you've got,' he said. 'Where are they holding him?'

Doolan nodded and smiled. 'That's about

the only bright spot,' he said. 'We do have some secret information. They're still holding him in Castlemore, but a friend on the inside gave us a tip this morning. They're going to move him to Belfast tomorrow night on the nine o'clock mail train. The whole thing's being done very quietly.'

Fallon nodded. 'Because they expect the glory boys to try something foolish.'

'You'll want the address of our local head-quarters in Castlemore,' Doolan said.

Fallon shook his head. 'No thanks,' he said. 'In the first place, I wouldn't feel safe working with a local group. There's still a reward of two thousand quid on my head. No – I've got to do it on my own. It's the only way.'

O'Hara nodded in approval. 'You're right, Martin. It's the only way, but you'll be needing a hidey hole of some sort.'

Fallon smiled. 'I've one or two of my own. Reliable ones from the old days.' He stood up and moved across to the window and looked out into the night.

'When will you go?' O'Hara asked.

Fallon lit another cigarette. 'In an hour or so.

I'll cross the border before morning. I can catch the milk train for Castlemore at Carlington.' He moved back to the fire and said, 'I'll give myself three days at the outside. If we get away with it I'll bring him straight here. No sense in getting him arrested on this side and put in that fine new detention camp they've got.' O'Hara nodded and Fallon sighed and said, 'I've been happy here, O'Hara. Happy for the first time in my life. If I ever get the chance I'll pay you back for doing this to me.'

O'Hara half-smiled and shook his head. 'No you won't,' he said. 'You're not the sort. Besides, you've never been happy here.' His eyes challenged Fallon calmly, surely, and Fallon suddenly knew that what the old man said was true.

He threw his cigarette into the fire and left the room. He quietly opened the bedroom door and went in. Mrs Rogan slept peacefully, her face calm and tranquil in the lamplight. Fallon opened a wardrobe and taking out a tweed suit, changed quickly. When he was ready, he took a battered rain hat and an old trench coat from a hook behind the door. For a moment he stood at the bedside looking down at the sleeping woman and then he turned down the lamp and moved to the window.

A bare half-mile away through the darkness was the border. Within a few hours be would be in great danger. The rain hammered endlessly on the glass and the wind called to him as it moaned through the trees. A sudden spark of excitement moved within him. He smiled softly in the darkness and turned and quietly left the room.

2

When the milk train pulled into Castlemore, Fallon was sleeping in a corner, his hat tilted over his eyes. An old farmer who had shared the compartment with him from Carlington, gave him a nudge and he came awake quickly and murmured his thanks.

The station was almost deserted and few passengers alighted. As he walked towards the barrier porters unloaded the milk churns noisily at the far end of the platform. A young policeman in the uniform of the Ulster Constabulary, revolver strapped high on his right side in black leather holster, chatted idly with the ticket-collector. His eyes flickered in a disinterested fashion over the passengers as they passed through, and he yawned hugely and lifted a hand to his mouth.

Fallon paused in the station entrance and looked across the square into a drift of fine rain. It had been easy. Almost too easy. He had crossed the border under cover of the darkness and rain, with no trouble at all. A brisk walk of half a mile had taken him into Carlington. Now here he was, back in enemy territory with almost every hand against him, and yet it was different somehow. There was not the old feeling of excitement, of tension. There was a flatness to this thing and an unreal quality as if it were a dream that he would soon wake from. He pulled his collar closely about his neck and struck out across the square into the rain.

He had not gone very far before he realized that he was being followed. It was still too early for many people to be about and he walked at an easy pace through the main shopping centre. He paused once to light a cigarette. As he cupped his hands around the match, he glanced casually back along the street and saw a man in a flat cap and brown leather motoring coat, halt abruptly and look into a shop window.

Fallon continued at the same easy pace. He took the next turning off the main street and began to walk faster. He crossed the road and turned into a narrow alley. Half-way along the alley he paused and looked back. The man in the brown leather coat was standing at the end watching him. Fallon began to walk briskly now. He felt almost lighthearted. At least he wasn't being followed by a policeman but by the rankest kind of amateur. He came out into a quiet street and flattened himself against the wall. His pursuer was running now, his footsteps echoing hollowly from the brick walls of the alley. When the steps were almost upon him, Fallon crossed the street and moved along the pavement.

There was no one about and the rain suddenly increased in volume until it bounced from the pavement in long lances and soaked heavily into the shoulders of his trench coat. A little way down the street he came to the entrance of a timber yard.

He hesitated and glanced back in time to see the man in the leather coat dodge back out of sight into the alley. The timber yard was deserted and wood was piled everywhere. The place was a jungle with narrow passages giving access to the heart of it. Fallon moved a few paces inside and took up position behind a convenient pyramid of oak planks.

Within a few moments his pursuer arrived. He paused in the entrance, glancing about him cautiously, and then moved forward. Fallon waited until he had passed his hiding place and then he stepped out and said, 'A dirty morning.' The man turned quickly and Fallon hit him hard under the breastbone.

The man sagged against a wall of planks, the breath whistling out of his body. His head jerked back in agony as he fought for air and his cap fell to the ground. He was only a boy, perhaps seventeen or eighteen, with red hair close-cropped to his skull. Fallon placed a hand on the boy's neck and pushed his head down relentlessly. He repeated the action several times and then stood back and waited.

After a moment the boy lifted a face that had turned bone-white and said with difficulty, 'You might give a fella a chance to explain himself.'

Fallon shrugged. 'I don't like being followed. Who are you, anyway?'

The boy picked up his cap. 'Will you look at that?' he said. 'Brand new last Monday and ruined.' He attempted to wipe mud from the cap with his sleeve, and finally cursed and replaced it on his head. 'Murphy is the name, Mr Fallon,' he said. 'Johnny Murphy. I was waiting for you at the station, but I had to be sure it was you.'

'And how were you sure?' Fallon asked.

'Oh, it was the beard, I think. I was told to look out for a man with a beard.' Here the boy laughed suddenly. 'To tell you the truth, Mr Fallon, I couldn't believe it was you. Hell, I thought you'd look different somehow.'

Fallon smiled briefly. 'People always do. It's a valuable asset in this game.' He took out a cigarette and lit it with difficulty in the rain. 'How did you know I was coming?' he said.

'That was easy,' Murphy told him. 'The Supervisor of the night shift in the telephone exchange at Carlington is a friend. He takes messages from the other side and passes them on.'

Fallon swore suddenly. 'I told Doolan I didn't want any help,' he said. 'This job's difficult enough without bringing kids into it.'

Murphy shrugged and said lightly, 'I may be a kid, but I'm all there is, Mr Fallon. The polis made a clean sweep yesterday. Lucky for me I hadn't actually joined the Organization. They didn't have a line on me.'

A vague feeling of alarm moved inside Fallon and suddenly he was afraid. The boy looked into his face steadily, the light smile firmly fixed on his mouth. After a few moments of silence Fallon relaxed and laughed. 'It's a proper bloody mess from the sound of it.'

Murphy nodded. 'What can you expect? They've got Rogan and they don't intend to lose him again. If ever there was a man they wanted to hang it's him.'

Something in the tone of the boy's voice

made Fallon look at him sharply. 'You don't like Rogan much, do you?'

The smile on the boy's face slipped a little. He forced it back into place. 'He's the Chief in Ulster and that's enough for me.'

For a moment Fallon gazed searchingly at him and then he smiled and said, 'Come on. We can't stay here any longer. The workmen will be arriving at any minute.'

They moved away through the heavy rain, down towards the main street, and Fallon thought about the situation. It didn't look good. In fact, it couldn't have been worse. 'Have they moved extra police in?' he said.

The boy shook his head. 'Not that I've noticed,' he said. 'Some detectives from Belfast arrived last night. They'll be Rogan's escort.'

'How many?' Fallon asked.

Murphy frowned. 'Four, I think, but there may be more. I can't be sure.'

Fallon nodded slowly. 'No, four would be about right. If they intend to do this thing quietly they won't want a six-foot peeler at every carriage window advertising the fact.'

They turned into the main road and

Murphy said, 'I don't see how you can get him out, Mr Fallon.'

Fallon laughed shortly. 'Neither do I at the moment,' he said. 'Still, I've got all day to think of something.' He smiled suddenly at Murphy and said, 'Perhaps it's a good thing you followed me after all.' The boy's face split into a wide grin and Fallon continued, 'Whatever happens I'm going to need a car.' He took out his wallet and extracted ten pounds. He handed the money to Murphy and said, 'Can you hire one all right?'

The boy nodded. 'Dead easy. Will you be needing anything else?'

'Such as?' Fallon said.

'Oh, explosives or arms. There's a load of stuff the polis didn't get to. It's in a safe place.'

Fallon nodded slowly. 'I'll have a look at it later,' he said. 'For the time being all I want you to do is get the car and have it ready and waiting.' He thought for a moment and added, 'You can get me a ticket for the train as well. I don't want to hang round that station too much.'

'A ticket to Belfast?' Murphy said.

Fallon shook his head. 'No, somewhere along the line.' He laughed. 'No sense in wasting money.' He looked out into the rain and up to the sky. 'Looks as if this lot's with us for the day.' He turned suddenly and clapped the boy on the shoulder. 'I'll meet you here at one o'clock.'

An expression of surprise showed on Murphy's face. 'But what will you do till then, Mr Fallon? It won't be safe for you on the streets.'

Fallon smiled. 'I'm going to visit an old friend.' His face hardened and he moved close to the boy and said, 'Don't try to follow me. This is someone I don't want to be involved with the Organization. Do you understand?'

The smile disappeared from the boy's face and he sobered up immediately. 'Anything you say, Mr Fallon.' He smiled again. 'One o'clock then. I won't be late.' He plunged into the rain and walked quickly away up the street.

For several minutes Fallon stood in the doorway watching until the boy had disappeared from sight and then he pulled up his collar and ventured into the rain himself.

He turned into a side street that took him away from the centre of the town. He twisted and turned through the back streets until he was completely satisfied that he was not being followed. Finally he came out into a quiet square that was surrounded on each side by terraces of tall, narrow Georgian houses. In one corner of the square there was a high wall in which was set an old, heavy timbered gate from which green paint peeled in long strips. He opened the gate and went inside.

He found himself in a walled garden. The place was a wilderness of sprawling weeds and grass grew unchecked across the path. Before him, through the rain, the brown bulk of an old house lifted to the leaden sky. He frowned in puzzlement as he surveyed the scene of desolation and then he slowly walked up the path to the door and jerked on the ancient bell-pull.

The sound jangled faintly in the hidden depths of the house and the echo was from another world. There was utter silence and after a few minutes he tried again. After a while he heard steps approaching the door.

There was the sound of bolts being withdrawn and the door opened slightly.

A young woman looked out at him. She was wearing an old camel-hair dressing gown and there was sleep in her eyes. 'What is it?' she said.

'Is Professor Murray at home?' Fallon asked her. A peculiar expression appeared on her face at once. He hastened to explain. 'I know it's early, but I'm just passing through and I promised to look him up. I'm an old student of his.'

For a moment the girl gazed fixedly at him and then she stepped back and opened the door wide. 'You'd better come in,' she said.

The door closed leaving the hall in semi-darkness. The air smelt musty and faintly unpleasant and as Fallon stumbled after her, he realized there was no carpet on the floor. She opened a door at the end of the passage and led the way into an old, stone-flagged kitchen. The room was warm and friendly and he took off his hat and unbuttoned his wet coat. 'This is better,' he said.

'Take your coat off,' the girl told him. She

went to a gas cooker in the corner and put a light under the kettle. Where the old-fashioned range had once stood there was now a modern coke-burning stove. She knelt down in front of it and began to clear ashes from the grate.

Fallon said, 'Is the Professor still in bed?'

She stood up and faced him. 'He died a few weeks ago,' she said. There was no change of expression on her face when she added, 'I'm his daughter – Anne.'

Fallon walked over to the window and stood staring out into the tangled garden and the rain. Behind him the girl busied herself at the cooker. After a while he turned round and said, 'He was the finest man I ever knew.'

There was ash on her hands from the grate. When she pushed back a loose tendril of her fair hair she smudged her forehead. 'He thought quite a bit about you, too, Mr Fallon.' She turned to the sink and rinsed her hands under the tap.

Fallon sat down in a chair by the table. 'How did you know who I was?' he asked.

'That scar,' she said. 'You staggered into

my father's flat in Belfast one night about ten years ago with your face laid open to the bone. He stitched it for you because you couldn't go to a doctor.' She turned towards him, a towel in her hand, and examined the scar. 'He didn't make a very good job of it, did he?'

'Good enough,' Fallon said. 'It kept me out of the hands of the police.'

She nodded. 'You and Philip Stuart were students together at Queen's before the war, weren't you?'

Fallon started in surprise. 'You know Phil Stuart?'

She smiled slightly as she put cups on the table. 'He drops in now and then. He only lives a couple of streets away. He's the County Inspector here, you know.'

Fallon slumped back in his chair with an audible sigh. 'No, I didn't know.'

As she poured tea out she went on, 'My father used to say he found it rather ironical that Stuart joined the Constabulary and you the other lot. He once told me that in you two he could see the whole history of Ireland.'

Fallon offered her a cigarette and smiled sadly. 'How right he was.' He stared into space, back into the past, and said slowly, 'He was a remarkable man. He used to shelter me when I was on the run and spend the night trying to make me see the error of my ways.' He straightened up in his chair and laughed lightly. 'Still, he used to see a lot of Stuart, as well. Poor Phil – if only he'd realized what was going on under his nose.'

Anne Murray sipped her tea and said quietly, 'What did you want with my father this time?'

Fallon shrugged. 'For once, nothing – except a chat. I hadn't seen him for several years, you know.'

'Yes, he wasn't even sure you were still alive. He thought you would have written to him if you had been.'

Fallon shook his head and explained. 'I've been buried in the wilds of Cavan,' he said. He grinned suddenly and poured himself another cup of tea. 'To tell you the truth I decided to change my ways. I've kept body and soul together by doing a bit of hack writing. I have a cottage about half a mile from the border. It's been most restful.'

She chuckled, deep down in her throat. 'I'm sure it has. But what did you find to take the place of the other thing?'

A sudden unease moved inside him and he forced a laugh. 'What other thing?'

'The thing that made you what you were; that made you live the kind of life you did for all those years.'

He stood up and paced restlessly about the room. The girl was getting too near the truth for comfort. After a few moments he swung round and said brightly, 'Anyway, what are you doing here? I hadn't realized you were so grown up. Didn't your father pack you off to some aunt in England after your mother died?'

'He did,' she said. 'Then I went to a boarding school. After that, Guy's Hospital in London. I'm a nurse,' she added simply.

He nodded. 'You came home for the funeral?'

She shook her head. 'I was here for a few days before he died. I've only stayed on to sell up. A lot of the furniture has gone already.' She shivered suddenly. 'I don't want any of it. I just want to get rid of everything and go away.'

For the first time grief showed starkly in her eyes and he put a hand on her shoulder. For a few moments they stayed together, tied by some mystical bond of sympathy, and then she moved slightly and he took his hand away. She looked up into his face and said quietly, 'What have you come for, Martin Fallon? Are you back at the old game?'

For a long moment their eyes were locked and then he sighed deeply. He moved across to his chair and sagged down into it. 'Yes, I'm back at the old game,' he said.

She nodded slowly and stared past him in an abstracted manner as if thinking deeply. After a moment she said, 'But why? That's what I can't understand. After all these years why come back to it?'

He shook his head several times. 'I don't know. I really don't know. I thought I was doing it for a woman who had already suffered too much, but now I'm not so sure.

Some impulse of self-destruction, perhaps. After all, why did I live the way I did for so many years?' He laughed suddenly. 'I don't think it was entirely for Ireland.'

The girl stood up and carried the cups to the sink. For a moment she paused, her back to him, and then she turned. 'I only know what my father told me. That you were a fine man ruined and a good mind wasted.' She shook her head slowly and repeated as if to herself, 'Wasted.'

At that moment the bell jangled sharply, waves of harsh sound breaking the silence that had followed her words.

For a brief second they stood looking at each other and then she opened the door and went swiftly along the dark passage. She was back in a moment. 'It's Philip Stuart,' she said. 'I can see him through the side window.'

Panic moved inside Fallon and for a moment a strange dizziness caused him to sway slightly. He staggered and almost lost his balance and then he was cold and calm again. His hand dipped inside his coat and came out clutching the Luger. 'What's he want?' he said and there was a deadness in his voice.

The girl grasped his wrist firmly and pushed the weapon down towards the floor. 'There will be none of that,' she said. 'He's been handling the sale of the house for me. He's a busy man at the moment and has to come when he can.' For a moment Fallon resisted and she put her face close to his and said, 'Put the gun away.'

He relaxed suddenly and slipped it back into the shoulder holster. 'I'm sorry,' he said.

She took him by the arm and led him across to another door. When she opened it he saw a flight of stairs. 'Straight up to the landing,' she said. 'The first room on the left is my bedroom. You can stay there until I come for you.' He tried to speak and then the bell rang again and she pushed him forward, throwing his hat and coat after him, and closed the door.

He found her room with no difficulty. A bed and an old dresser seemed to be the only furniture and a few suitcases stood against one wall. He sat down on the edge of the bed.

His hands were trembling and after a few moments his whole body began to shake. He let his body fall back against the pillows, his hands clasped together, and closed his eyes as a sob rose in his throat. 'I'm afraid,' he said, half aloud. 'I'm scared to death. I've lost my nerve.' He lay there, his body shaking, and then after a while he felt drowsy. The room was quiet and still and there was the faint womanly smell of the girl upon the bedclothes. Quite suddenly he relaxed. She seemed to come very close to him, bringing with her an inexpressible comfort, and then the tiredness came to him. His head dropped gently to one side as he drifted into darkness.

He came awake quickly from a dreamless sleep and lay staring at the ceiling. For a few moments he couldn't remember where he was. Awareness came to him and he swung his feet to the floor and looked at his watch. It was almost noon. He cursed softly and stood up, and then he realized with surprise that his shoes had been taken off and were standing neatly at the side of the bed. He frowned in puzzlement and sat down again to put them on. His coat and hat had disappeared and he spent several moments looking for them before he went to the door and opened it cautiously. The house was quiet. He advanced along the passage and began to descend the back stairs.

Faintly from the kitchen came sounds of music. For a moment he hesitated at the door and then he opened it and went in. The music came from a wireless on a shelf in the corner. The girl was standing at the gas cooker stirring something in a pan. She turned quickly and said, without smiling, 'You're awake.'

Fallon nodded. 'Why did you let me sleep?'

She shrugged. 'You looked as though you needed it.' She moved across to the table and spooned stew on to a plate. 'You'd better sit down and have this.' She had changed into a tweed skirt and green, woollen jumper. Somehow she looked older, more sure of herself.

Fallon sat down and said, 'I'll have to be quick. I've got an appointment at one o'clock.'

As he ate, the girl sat on the opposite side of the table, a cup of tea in her hands, and watched him. After a while she said, 'Stuart's found me a buyer for the house. It won't fetch much – it's too run down for that – but it will be better than nothing.' Fallon nodded and went on eating. For some strange reason he couldn't think of anything to say. There was an air of tension in the air as if something was going to snap at any moment. Suddenly the girl leaned forward and said, 'You're here to get that fellow Rogan, aren't you?'

He paused, the spoon halfway to his mouth, and looked at her searchingly. 'Who told you that?'

She leaned back, satisfied. 'I just put two and two together. It had to be something special to bring you back. I should have thought of it before.'

'Did Stuart say anything?' Fallon asked.

She shook her head. 'Nothing special. He mentioned Rogan in passing. Said they would be moving him to Belfast soon. I suddenly realized there must be a connection.'

Fallon pushed the empty plate away from him. 'That was nice,' he said.

She leaned across the table again and there was anger sparking in her eyes. 'You damned fool. You'll get yourself killed this time. And for what? For a cold-blooded murderer who deserves to hang.'

He shook his head and shrugged. 'Some people might say he was a soldier.'

She laughed harshly. 'Don't talk rubbish. He's a dirty little terrorist who shoots people in the back.'

He didn't try to answer her because he knew that she was more than half right. For a few moments he looked into her blazing, angry eyes and then he dropped his gaze and began to trace a pattern in the table cloth with the handle of his knife. 'Rogan has a mother,' he said. 'She's lost a husband and a son already. Both shot down fighting for the Cause. She wants him back. He's all she has left.'

Anne Murray gave a little moan and jumped up suddenly. 'It's always the women who suffer,' she said. For a moment she stood with her head lowered and then she shook it slowly from side to side. 'It won't do,' she said. 'It's not a good enough reason.'

He got up from the table and took down his hat and coat from the rack where she had put them to dry. 'I must go,' he said.

She moved slowly towards him and paused when their bodies were almost touching. There was iron in her voice when she spoke. 'That woman isn't the reason you came, is it?' He made no reply and she raised her voice and said demandingly, 'Is it?'

For a moment there was a great silence as they stood close together staring into each other's eyes, and then she swayed suddenly and he reached out to steady her. 'A man ought to finish what he starts,' he said.

She nodded wearily. 'Men!' There was almost a loathing in her voice. 'Men and their honour and their stupid games.'

She came with him to the door. The rain was still falling steadily and remorselessly into the sodden ground. He belted his coat around him and pulled his hat down over his eyes. For a moment they stood together there on the top step and then a sob broke in her throat and she pushed him off the step, and said angrily, 'Go on – go to your death, you fool.'

The door slammed into place and for a moment he stood looking at it, and then he turned and walking down through the tangled garden, let himself out into the rain-swept square.

3

When Fallon reached the meeting place he found Murphy waiting for him. The boy was sitting behind the wheel of an old Austin reading a newspaper. Fallon walked quickly round to the other side of the car and opened the door. Murphy looked up, an expression of alarm on his face. He smiled with relief. 'God help us, Mr Fallon. I thought you were the polis.'

Suddenly Fallon felt desperately sorry for the boy. He wanted to tell him that this was how it would always be. That there was no romance and no adventure in it at all. That from now on he would live with fear. But he said none of these things. He looked into the boy's eager, reckless young face and saw himself twenty years ago. He smiled and said, 'Do you smoke?' Murphy nodded and they lit cigarettes and sat back in comfort while the rain drummed on the roof.

'Do you like the car?' Murphy asked. Fallon nodded, and the boy went on. 'I got it a bit cheaper, but I thought it would be less conspicuous. Did I do right?'

Fallon laughed lightly. 'You used your head,' he said. 'And that's the only thing that keeps men like us out of the hands of the police.'

Murphy flushed with pleasure. 'Will you have a look at that stuff I was telling you about, Mr Fallon?'

Fallon nodded and the boy took the car away from the kerb in a sudden burst of speed. 'Steady on!' Fallon told him. 'No sense in being picked up for dangerous driving.'

Murphy slowed down a little and they proceeded along the main street through light traffic at a steady pace. Fallon leaned back in his seat and tipped his hat down over his eyes. Until this moment he had given the problem of how he was to get Rogan off the train no immediate thought. He considered the business soberly. At first sight it was impossible. There would be at least four detectives with Rogan. They would be well armed and in a reserved compartment. Possibly even in a reserved coach. He shook his head. It looked bad and it was one of those tricky jobs which depended on circumstances and couldn't be properly planned beforehand. The car braked to a halt and Murphy switched off the engine. 'We're here. Mr Fallon,' he said.

They were parked in a back street beside a high stone wall, and beyond the wall the tower of a church lifted into the sky. Fallon looked out in puzzlement. 'Are you sure this is it?' he said.

The boy grinned. 'Don't worry, Mr Fallon. We're at the right place. The safest place in the world.' He produced a bunch of keys from his pocket and got out of the car. There was a solid-looking door set in the face of the stone wall. He opened it with one of the keys and motioned Fallon through.

Fallon found himself standing at the back of a graveyard. A forest of monuments and gravestones reared out of the ground on all sides and the church stood at the far side, firmly rooted into the ground. Murphy led the way towards the church, picking his route through the graves with care. He halted at a small wooden door that was half sunk into the ground at the base of the church walls so that three small steps led down to it. Murphy took out the bunch of keys again and selecting one of them, tried the door. It failed to open. He cursed and tried again. At the fourth attempt the door opened and he disappeared inside. Fallon followed him cautiously.

He found himself in the half-darkness of a stone vault. Great arching ribs of stone supported the ceiling and the only light seeped through an iron grill that looked out on to the graveyard. There was a click and Murphy switched on the light. 'It's got everything this place, Mr Fallon,' he said. 'Electric light and running water.' He pointed to the steady trickle of rain that was seeping through the iron grill and down the wall, and laughed.

'Where are we?' Fallon demanded.

'Church of St Nicholas,' Murphy told him. 'In the vaults. No one ever comes in here. We're quite safe.'

'Are you sure about that?' Fallon said.

'Look for yourself,' Murphy pointed to a truckle bed and several boxes which stood in the far corner. 'That stuff's been there for over a year now. No one ever comes down here.'

Fallon raised a hand. 'All right, don't get worked up. I believe you.' He looked around the quiet vault and sighed. 'It seems a dirty trick to use a place like this.'

Murphy's face sobered immediately. 'I used to think that,' he said, 'but it was Rogan's idea. He said the end justified the means.'

Fallon laughed grimly. 'It always does. You know, the more I hear about Mr Patrick Rogan the less I like him.' He unbuttoned his coat and moved across to the boxes. 'All right, let's have a look at this stuff you've got here.'

In the boxes he found a formidable collection of explosives. In the first box were hand-grenades and clips of ammunition.

The second contained belts of plastic explosive. It was the third box that Fallon found interesting. 'Where did they get this one?' he said.

Murphy came and had a look. 'Oh, that was a job they did one night when there were troops camped just outside the town. They broke into the ammunition store. Rogan was furious. He said they'd taken the wrong box. Why, what's in there?'

Fallon laughed. 'Smoke bombs. I can see what he meant. Not a great deal of use in our kind of work.' He started to close the box again and then hesitated. 'I wonder,' he said, and there was a faraway look in his eyes.

'What good would them things be, Mr Fallon?' Murphy said.

Fallon smiled softly and took one of the smoke bombs out and hefted it in his hand. 'This might just be the solution.' He sat on the edge of the bed and explained. 'The things are automatic. You break this fuse at the end and a chemical action starts instantly. I've seen them work. Within a matter of seconds they give off thick clouds of black smoke. What sort of effect would it have, do you think, if I let one of these things go to work on that train?'

'Jesus help us!' Murphy said. 'There'd be a panic. People would think the train was on fire.'

'Exactly!' Fallon murmured. 'Everybody would panic, the women would be near hysterical. The corridors crammed with people. Just the right conditions in which to rescue a man.'

'It can't fail,' Murphy said in awe. 'God help us, you're a genius, Mr Fallon.'

'Don't talk nonsense,' Fallon said. 'Have you got a map of the district?' Murphy produced one from his inside pocket and Fallon spread it out on the bed and examined it. After a few minutes he said, 'Now listen carefully. About ten miles out of Castlemore on the east side of the railway track is a wood. Do you know it?' Murphy examined the map and nodded and Fallon went on, 'I want you to be there with the car from nine-fifteen onwards. No earlier because

I don't want you hanging about looking conspicuous.'

'Don't you think it's a bit close to town?' Murphy asked.

Fallon shook his head. 'Absolute surprise is the one thing that will bring this off. Even if they do expect trouble I don't think they'll be looking for it so soon. They'd be thinking in terms of someone trying to board the train at one of the smaller stations along the line.' He sighed. 'Anyway, that's it. You never can tell what's going to happen in this game, but at least this scheme has a chance.'

'What happens afterwards – if it does come off,' Murphy said. 'Do we make a run for the border?'

Fallon shook his head. 'That's what they all do,' he said, 'and that's why they get caught. We'll come straight back here and lie low for at least three days.'

Murphy took out a battered wallet and extracted a railway ticket. 'There you are,' he said. 'A single to Dunveg. That's three stops up the line.'

'Good lad!' As he put the ticket away

Fallon said, 'What do you do for a living, Johnny? Today, for instance?'

The boy laughed and shrugged his shoulders. 'I'm lucky there. My parents are dead. My father left us a grocery shop in one of the back streets. Kathleen – that's my sister – she runs it. I'm supposed to help her, but I told her I was busy today. Besides, business will be slack. Always is on a wet day.'

Fallon nodded and stood up. 'We'll take a run out to the scene of the crime,' he said. 'If you know a good pub on the way where we can get a bite to eat, stop at it. We've got all the time in the world.'

They found a quiet place just off the main road outside Castlemore and they parked the car and had a meal. Afterwards they followed the main road, parallel to the railway track, until they came to the place Fallon had picked out on the map. There was a track into the wood running between two ancient stone gateposts. The gates had long since disappeared and Murphy turned the car in between them and ran a little way along the track before cutting the motor. 'Couldn't be better,' he said. 'I can park up here tonight away from the main road.'

'Wait for me here,' Fallon said. He got out of the car and trudged along the narrowing path that led in amongst the trees. Within a couple of minutes he passed through the wood and came out on to the side of the track. For several minutes he stood in the cold rain looking at the track in an abstracted fashion. He felt completely deflated and drained of all emotion. My God, he thought, I'm not even excited. He sighed and a half-smile came to his lips. 'Must be getting old,' he said softly, and turned and went down through the trees back towards the car.

It was about four-thirty when they reached the church again. Murphy turned off the engine and Fallon said, 'Give me the keys to the doors.' The boy took the two necessary keys off the ring and handed them across and Fallon went on, 'I want you to park the car somewhere and go home now. I don't want your sister to start worrying about where you might be.'

'She doesn't know I'm working for the Organization,' Murphy told him.

'Then keep it that way,' Fallon said. 'Go home, have your tea and read a book or something. Leave the house eight-fifteen. Drive straight to the rendezvous.'

'What about you?' the boy said. 'Don't you want me to pick you up?'

Fallon shook his head and got out of the car. He closed the door and leaned in at the window. 'I'm going to hole up here until train time. I'll go to the station on my own.'

Murphy reversed the car and Fallon moved towards the door in the wall. As he stopped to insert the key the boy's clear young voice said softly, 'Good luck, Mr Fallon. Up the Republic!'

Fallon turned and half-raised one hand. 'Good luck, lad. If that train doesn't stop, go home and forget you ever heard of me.'

'No fear of that,' Murphy said with a reckless, confident smile and the car roared away in a shower of mud.

The vault was cold and dreary. Fallon lay on the truckle bed and stared at the ceiling and smoked a cigarette. The grey October evening drew to a close and the light dimmed as it filtered through the iron grill. Faintly, from somewhere in the depths of the church, came the sound of an organ, and a little later the brittle sweetness of boys' voices raised in song. He felt no particular dread at the prospect of action to come. He felt curiously detached from the whole thing as if he wasn't there at all but somewhere outside, looking in on all this.

He began to think of Anne Murray and of what she had said. She was right, of course, but he found that he wasn't thinking so much of her words as of the girl herself. He remembered how she had looked when she opened the door, with the fair hair tumbled over her brow and the sleep heavy in her eyes. He smiled softly in the darkness. She had the kind heart. She had found him sleeping on her bed and had taken off his shoes without waking him. But why had she got so angry with him? He couldn't understand that at all. There had been no need for hot words. For a brief moment her green eyes seemed to challenge him out of the darkness, and when he turned his head on the pillow it was as though he was back on her bed, surrounded by that elusive fragrance that was peculiarly her own.

He was sitting between two men in a railway compartment. The train was travelling at a nightmare speed, rocking and lurching from side to side. Suddenly through the window he could see the wood, but the train didn't stop. The men in the carriage began to laugh and he looked down and saw the hand-cuffs on his wrists and he turned to the man on his left and cried, 'It's a mistake! It's Rogan you want – not me. It's a mistake.' The man continued to laugh and as he laughed he changed into a judge in black cap and Fallon cried out and said, 'It's a mistake I tell you. It's Patrick Rogan you want – not me.' And then everybody began to laugh at him, heads thrown back, and the laughter mounted into the skies and he screamed as he felt the rope touch his neck.

He awakened, bathed in perspiration, and lay, panting and gasping for breath, for several moments. He had been dreaming. It had been only a dream. A sob issued from his mouth and he swung his legs to the floor and sat on the edge of the bed, head resting in his hands. It was completely still and quiet, and suddenly he jumped to his feet and looked at his watch. The luminous hands pointed to eight-fifteen. He sighed with relief and stumbled through the darkness to the switch in the corner. There was a piece of blanketing lying on the floor by the grill, and when he picked it up he saw that it fitted on two hooks to make a primitive curtain. He got ready quickly. He found a canvas grip behind the boxes and packed half-a-dozen smoke bombs into it. He checked the action of his Luger, reloaded it carefully, and then put on his hat and coat and let himself out into the graveyard.

It was still raining heavily as he walked through the town towards the station. There was very little traffic about and few people on the streets. The station restaurant was full of people driven in by the rain, and Fallon smiled to himself. That was a break, anyway. He got a cup of tea at the counter and squeezed his way through the crowd until he was standing by a window that looked out on to the platform and the ticket barrier.

The train was standing at the platform, a wisp of steam drifting up between its wheels. He glanced at his watch. It was only twenty-to-nine. He sipped his tea slowly and waited. At five-to-nine his patience was rewarded. A large dark car drove into the station entrance and stopped a few yards from the ticket barrier. The police were large men, in shabby raincoats and trilby hats, but the man that walked handcuffed between two of them was small and broad, with dark hair swept back from a white face. He was wearing an open-necked shirt, the collar spread out over a tweed jacket.

Fallon pushed his way out of the restaurant and hurried across to the barrier. As the detectives passed through with their prisoner, he offered his ticket to the collector and smiled pleasantly at the uniformed constable who was leaning against the barrier. 'Excuse me, but this *is* the Belfast train, isn't it?' he said in his finest English accent. The constable nodded and winked broadly at the ticket collector. As Fallon moved away they both laughed.

Rogan and his escort got into the coach next to the guard's van, and Fallon walked quickly along the platform, glancing eagerly into the windows as if looking for an empty compartment. As he reached the last coach he sighed with relief. Rogan and the detectives were settling down in a reserved compartment, but the rest of the coach was occupied by ordinary passengers. Porters were running along the platform slamming doors shut, and Fallon boarded the train quickly and passed along the corridor. Rogan and his escort were in the end compartment and Fallon took a seat in the next one to it. The only other occupant was a large, fat gentleman who looked like a commercial traveller. He was already sleeping peacefully in a corner seat.

For a moment there was silence and then the whistle blew. The train jerked a few times and began to move out of the station. Within five minutes they had left Castlemore behind in the darkness and were speeding through the rain towards Belfast. Fallon lit a cigarette and drew the smoke deeply into his lungs. He felt completely calm and fatalistic about the whole thing. He glanced at his watch and made a swift calculation. They must have covered just over half the distance to the wood. He stood up and passed quickly along the corridor, glancing briefly into the next compartment as he did so. Three of the detectives were playing cards and Rogan was handcuffed to the other one. They had taken his shoes off and he sat with his feet propped up on the opposite seat.

Fallon went into the toilet and closed the door. He counted up to twenty slowly and then opened the door to go back to his compartment. He walked straight into one of the detectives. The man laughed and started to apologize and Fallon smiled pleasantly, and then recognition flickered into the other's eyes. 'Fallon!' he said. 'Martin Fallon!'

In that split second of recognition Fallon reflected bitterly that you could never trust in any plan because the unexpected always happened. At the same moment, before the detective could raise the alarm, he raised a knee into his crutch and rammed his fist into his stomach. The man's face turned purple and, as he keeled over, Fallon hit him again in the back of the neck and dragged him into the toilet.

He pushed the man down in an inert heap in the corner and backed out, closing the door. There was no time to lose now. He moved back quickly to his own compartment, and taking down the canvas grip, hurried to the far end of the coach. He went into the toilet there and closed the door. He opened the grip and took out two smoke bombs which he slipped into the side pockets of his trench coat and then he took out another, broke the fuse, and dropped it into the used towel container. As he opened the door and backed out black smoke began to gush forth.

He had noticed an empty compartment half-way along the coach. As he passed it, he took out another bomb, broke the fuse, and tossed it up on to the luggage rack. He did the same in his own compartment where the fat man still slept peacefully in the corner. He passed the end compartment and noticed that the remaining three detectives were still playing cards and then, behind him, he heard a woman scream, high and piercing, and a man cried out, 'Fire! Fire!'

Fallon didn't hesitate for a moment. He pulled the communication cord that stretched above the carriage door and tossed another bomb into the entrance to the next carriage. He opened the door and stepped out on to the running board as the train began to slow.

The rain lashed his face and the wind pushed him against the side of the train. He gripped the handrail firmly and slammed the door back into place with all his strength. Then he reached up and secured a grip on the edge of the roof and pulled himself along until he was just able to see into the end compartment. Two of the detectives had disappeared, leaving Rogan handcuffed to the third. The shouts and screams seemed to rise to a crescendo as the train lurched and skidded to a halt and the detective turned to Rogan, his face white with fear as smoke swept into the compartment. He shouted something that Fallon could not hear and taking out a key, unlocked the handcuff from his left wrist. He snapped it over Rogan's free wrist, chaining his wrists together, and then, as another cloud of black smoke swept into the compartment, he turned towards the window.

As the train ground to a halt, Fallon moved back quickly to the carriage door and dropped down on to the track. He crouched low as the window of the compartment was pulled down and the detective and Rogan leaned out, coughing and gasping as the fresh air cut into their lungs. Fallon jumped up and caught hold of the detective by his coat lapels. The man was taken completely by surprise. His body dipped over the sill and he fell heavily to the track. He groaned and tried to get up and Fallon hit him in the side of the neck. He crouched down and quickly ran his hands through the man's pockets. His searching fingers fastened over the handcuff keys and he straightened up and said urgently, 'For God's sake, Rogan! What are you waiting for?'

Rogan was only half-way out of the window and Fallon reached up impatiently and dragged him bodily down. Rogan scrambled to his feet cursing. 'I was looking for my bloody shoes,' he said. 'The bastards took them off.'

'To hell with your shoes,' Fallon snarled. 'Let's get moving.' He pushed Rogan forward and they began to run back along the track towards the wood. As he ran, Fallon took out the two remaining smoke bombs which he had carried in his pockets, broke the fuses, and dropped them. Within a few moments the smoke rose behind them, blocking the lights of the train from view.

Both men ran without speaking, saving their breath for the running. Fallon led the way, crashing through the undergrowth like a wild beast, never stopping, his arms raised to protect his face from the flailing branches. He stumbled out on to the track that led down through the trees and paused. Rogan cannoned into him with a curse and then a voice from the darkness said, 'Is it yourself, Mr Fallon?'

Fallon ran forward and bumped into Johnny Murphy. 'Thank God!' he said. 'Get that motor running and let's be out of here.' He opened the rear door of the Austin and pushed Rogan in before him. The engine roared into life and the car reversed quickly down the track and turned into the main road. Within a few seconds they were speeding through the night towards Castlemore.

Fallon took out a packet of cigarettes and lit one with shaking hands. He leaned back in the seat and sighed contentedly. 'Thank God that's over.'

Murphy laughed excitedly. 'Didn't I say you were the genius, Mr Fallon? Sure I knew you'd get him off that train.'

Fallon laughed and there was a slight crack in his voice. 'It was so ridiculously easy. No shooting, no killing. Just a few little smoke bombs.'

Rogan seemed to have recovered his wind. He leaned forward. 'Are you Martin Fallon?' There was incredulity in his voice. 'Hell, I thought you were dead.'

There was the hint of a sneer in his voice and Murphy said angrily, 'A damn good job for you he wasn't.'

'Keep your shirt on,' Rogan said. He turned to Fallon. 'Did you get the keys off that fella?' Fallon produced the keys and unlocked the handcuffs. Rogan sighed with pleasure. 'God, how I hate wearing those things. There's something final about the feel of them when they're clipped on.' He laughed harshly. 'Aye, but I've fooled them. I've shown them they can't push Pat Rogan around and get away with it.'

Fallon was faintly disgusted. There was something unpleasant about the man. He decided that the sooner they parted company the better he would like it. 'Would you like a cigarette?' he said.

Rogan shook his head and said ungraciously, 'I don't smoke. I could do with some bloody shoes though. My socks are in shreds.'

Fallon forced himself to sound pleasant. 'Sorry about that,' he said. 'Johnny can get you a pair tomorrow if you give him the size.'

Rogan grunted and made no reply. Already they were running through the outskirts of Castlemore and Murphy slowed down and followed the other vehicles quietly into the

town. It was a little after ten when he cut
the engine at the back of the church. Fallon
unlocked the gate and led the way through
the graveyard. The rain had increased in
volume again and Rogan was soaked to the
skin by the time they reached the shelter of
the vault. Fallon switched on the light and
started to strip off his wet coat. Rogan
groaned. 'Christ, is there no better place than
this?'

Fallon shrugged and said evenly, 'You're
lucky to be here. It's the safest place for the
moment.'

Rogan cursed and turned on the boy. 'Why
the hell can't we hide up at your place?' he
demanded.

The boy flushed. He tried to speak, but
Fallon cut in and said coldly, 'Because I say so.'

Rogan turned angrily. 'And who the hell
are you to be giving the orders? I'm the Chief
in Ulster.'

Fallon laughed sharply. 'You mean you
were.' He walked forward until he was
standing very close to Rogan. He looked
steadily down into the small man's eyes.

'Don't try to play games with me. Rogan. You and I both know why I'm here. There was some question of a deal, I understand.' A shutter clicked in Rogan's eyes and Fallon continued, 'You'll stay here for three days and you'll do as I say. After we've crossed the border you can hang yourself for all I care.' He smiled and said softly, 'You see, I don't happen to like you.'

Rogan smiled mirthlessly, his lips drawn back to show even white teeth. There was hate in his eyes as he said, 'All right, Mr Fallon. Anything you say. You're the boss – for the present.' He turned to Murphy. 'Get me a pair of shoes in the morning, kid. Size nine. Brogues will do fine.'

Murphy nodded and moved towards the door. Fallon followed and stood for a moment, a hand on the boy's shoulder. 'You did a good job tonight,' he said. The boy flushed and an expression of blazing pride shone in his face. He tried to speak and then he turned quickly and went out into the night.

Fallon went over to the bed and took two

of the blankets. 'You can have the bed for tonight,' he said.

Rogan nodded and began to take off his jacket. Suddenly he swung round and said, 'We got off on the wrong foot, you and I. I'm sorry. I was a bit worked up. Everything happened so damned quickly.'

Fallon didn't believe a word of it. 'That's all right,' he said, in a non-committal tone.

Rogan sat down on the edge of the bed. 'Come to think of it, I don't mind hanging round this town for a few days,' he said. 'There's one bastard here I'd like to even the score with before I leave.'

Fallon paused in the act of spreading his blankets on the floor in the corner. 'And who would that be?' he said.

Rogan got into bed and pulled the blankets up to his chin. 'The bloody County Inspector,' he said savagely. 'Stuart they call him. Ever since he got the job last year he's hounded me from every safe hole I had. He was the one who lifted me three days ago.' There was a deadly coldness in his voice when he added, 'I'll fix Mr County Inspector Stuart before I go.'

Fallon made no reply. He switched off the light and wrapping himself in the blankets, settled down in the corner. Rogan sickened him. What type are they getting in the Organization now, he asked himself? And then he smiled sadly and decided that perhaps the type had not changed. Perhaps Martin Fallon was the one who had changed. Whatever happened he was going to have to keep an eye on Rogan, that was obvious. A thought struck him and he smiled and reached for his jacket. The shoulder holster was sewn into place just under his left armhole. He withdrew the Luger quietly and placed it under his blankets, close to his right hand.

He used his jacket as a pillow and leaned back and waited for sleep. The day's events rushed through the darkness before him, spinning round and round like a piece of film with all the scenes wrongly joined together. He was surprised to discover that, out of all that had happened, his encounter with Anne Murray stood out most clearly. He smiled again and shook his head. One thing was certain. She would certainly know what he had been up to when she read the morning papers. He felt calm and contented with no fear at all. Sufficient unto the day, he thought. We'll see what happens tomorrow. He turned his head to one side and went to sleep as calmly as a young child.

4

Fallon slept lightly. When he first awakened and checked his watch it was shortly after five. He was cold and stiff and his limbs ached from contact with the stone floor. He lay in the darkness listening to the rain and the wind as it moaned through the graveyard. After a while he drifted into sleep again.

He became aware that someone was prodding him and opened his eyes, at the same time feeling for the butt of the Luger. Johnny Murphy squatted beside him. The blanket was down from the iron grill and a grey light seeped into the room. 'Is it still raining?' Fallon said softly.

The boy nodded. 'It hasn't let up all night.'

He held up a large thermos flask. 'Get some of this into you, Mr Fallon. It'll do you a power of good.'

Fallon swallowed some of the hot liquid. It was coffee, strong and good. He sat up and rested his back against the wall. 'How's our friend doing?' he said.

Murphy grunted in disgust. 'Fast asleep. I don't like that man at all, Mr Fallon. It's the look in his eyes puts me off.'

Fallon smiled softly. 'Can't say I blame you.' He looked at his watch. It was a little after eight. 'You're early enough,' he said. 'What's the news in the outside world?'

Murphy produced a paper and said, with a shake of the head, 'It isn't so good, Mr Fallon and that's a fact. They're on to you. They haven't had enough time to get much into the papers, but I listened to the seven o'clock news on the radio. You were recognized.'

Fallon swore softly. 'Hell, I forgot about the damned peeler who bumped into me in the corridor. He recognized me. I had to dump him in the toilet. What did it say on the news?'

'They spoke about you mostly. Gave a full description. Described the scar and said you were wearing a beard now.'

Fallon laughed tightly. 'Well, that's the first thing that has to go then. A pity. I'd grown rather fond of this beard.'

The boy smiled. 'I thought of that myself. I've brought you the necessaries.' He took a bundle from one pocket and unwrapped it. Inside was a razor and a tube of shaving cream. 'I've put a new blade in it,' he added. 'I thought you'd probably need it.'

Fallon rubbed some of the cream well into his beard and started to shave it off. It was a painful business without hot water and he winced and cursed softly several times while Murphy sat back on his heels and watched him. It took about fifteen minutes to make a reasonable job and he put the razor down with a sigh of relief and wiped his face with a handkerchief. 'How do I look?' he said.

Murphy whistled. 'I wouldn't have recognized you. Mind you, there's still the scar, but you look ten years younger.'

Before Fallon could reply there was a groan

from the bed and Rogan pushed himself up on one elbow. He looked across at them, rubbing a hand across his eyes, and said, 'What the hell are you two up to? What time is it?'

Fallon stood up and moved across the room. 'No need to worry,' he said. 'It's about eight o'clock.' He turned to the boy. 'Better give him some coffee.'

Rogan stared at him in surprise. 'What's happened to the beard?' he said.

Fallon shrugged and handed him the newspaper. 'If you look in the stop press you'll see why. They're on to me. They broadcast a description on the radio.'

Rogan read the item in the stop press column and snorted with disgust. 'There's hardly a mention of me here,' he said. 'It's all about you.'

For a moment Fallon had an insane desire to laugh, but he controlled himself with an effort. 'Obviously we're going to have to stick close to this place. Perhaps for longer than we thought. They'll raise the whole countryside.'

Rogan laughed harshly. 'They needn't think they'll take me again so easily.' He yawned and continued, 'Well, as we don't seem to be in any particular rush to get out of this hole I might as well go back to sleep again.' He turned his face to the wall and pulled the blanket up about his neck.

Fallon went to the door with the boy. 'You'd better stay away for the rest of the day,' he said. 'I'm not happy about this system. It only needs someone to see you coming through that graveyard and we've had it.'

The boy nodded. 'I can't come back until this evening anyway. I've got to help Kathleen in the shop.'

Fallon slapped him on the shoulder. 'Then do that. We don't want her to get suspicious. What about the car?'

'I hired it for three days,' Murphy said. 'Shall I take it back?'

Fallon thought for a moment and then shook his head. 'No, hang on to it. It might be useful if we have to get out of here in a hurry.' He opened the door and gave the boy a push. 'Go on! Off with you! I'll see you

85

sometime between five and six.' Murphy flashed him a smile and hurried away through the rain.

When Fallon went back to his makeshift bed he found a brown paper parcel on the floor. He smiled. The boy must have forgotten to tell him about it. Inside he found sandwiches, two or three apples and some oranges. Also a pair of cheap shoes for Rogan. He ate a little of the fruit and lay back on the blankets and stared up at the vaulted ceiling, and after a while he followed Rogan's example and went to sleep again.

When he awakened, Rogan was sitting on the floor by the boxes with some of the weapons spread out around him. He had a length of string which appeared to be fastened to one of the hand grenades and he stood up and backed away, paying the string out as he went. 'What are you supposed to be doing?' Fallon asked.

Rogan looked over his shoulder and grinned. 'Just experimenting,' he said. 'This is a good way of exploding a grenade by remote control. The string is attached to the pin – pull the string and up she goes.'

Fallon frowned. 'For God's sake mind you don't pull the string now.' There was an obvious irritation in his voice which he made no attempt to conceal. He was getting a little tired of Patrick Rogan.

The small man shrugged, an expression of unconcern on his face. 'What's the matter? Don't tell me the great Martin Fallon is losing his nerve?' He laughed malevolently and picked up a canvas belt. 'Now this is the great stuff – plastic gelignite. It's even waterproof. I've pulled off some good stunts in my time using this.'

Fallon gazed at him in disgust. There was something unclean about him, something completely inhuman. 'For Christ's sake keep your mouth shut if that's all you can talk about,' he said coldly and lay back against the blankets again.

The rest of the day passed slowly. The two men only spoke when it was necessary and Rogan paced backwards and forwards over the stone flags, growing more and more impatient as the day advanced. Fallon slept again during the afternoon, and the evening was drawing in when he awakened. He glanced at his watch. It was almost five o'clock. Rogan was standing at the grill looking out into the graveyard. 'What's the weather like?' Fallon said.

The small man spoke without turning round. 'Bloody awful! I don't think it's ever going to stop raining.'

The room seemed smaller as the shadows lengthened in the corners and Fallon got up and walked across to the door and opened it slightly. The rain hammered down from the leaden sky, splashing deliberately into the mounded graves. He lit a cigarette and stood looking across the gravestones down to the wall, dimly seen in the gloom. The graves were uncared for, for the most part, with grass and weeds running wild, and all at once he was filled with a terrible sadness at the emptiness and the futility of life. There was a creaking of rusty hinges as the door in the wall opened and Murphy hurried through the gravestones towards him.

Fallon opened the door and the boy slipped inside. His face was white with excitement.

'Jesus, help us, Mr Fallon! I've never seen so many peelers as I have today. The town's crawling with them.'

'Have you got another newspaper?' Fallon demanded. The boy nodded and produced one from his pocket. There was nothing new in it. The story was headlines now and there were pictures of Fallon and Rogan side by side. The one of Fallon was not a very good one and he grunted in satisfaction. 'That's a lousy photo,' he said. He passed the paper across to Rogan and added thoughtfully, 'I wonder why they've concentrated the police in Castlemore. You'd think they would be combing the countryside.'

Rogan rapped out an oath and threw the newspaper away from him in a rage. 'It's that bastard Stuart,' he said. 'The clever one, he is. I'll fix him before I'm through.'

'For Christ's sake cut that out and let's discuss something important,' Fallon said, and then a blast of cold air hit him in the back of the neck as the door creaked open behind him.

Fallon turned slowly as a voice said,

'What's going on here? What's the meaning of this?'

A small, shrivelled old man in a clerical collar and shabby black raincoat was standing just inside the door. There was complete silence as he looked at them and then recognition dawned in his eyes. 'Fallon!' he said. 'Fallon and Rogan.' Very deliberately he brushed past them and stood looking down at the explosives in the boxes by the bed. For a moment he remained with his head bowed and then he turned and there was pain and anger in his voice. 'How dare you!' he said. 'How dare you use God's house for your filthy work. Gunmen, murderers, the lot of you.'

'For God's sake, Father,' Fallon began, but the old man cut in on him.

'I'm going to phone for the police.' His voice was ice-cold now, but his whole body was trembling with rage. 'That gives you five minutes at the most to get out.'

As the priest started forward Rogan moved quickly and grabbed him by the arm. 'Not so fast,' he snarled. 'You aren't going anywhere.'

All the dislike that Fallon had been nursing,

all the hatred and the disgust at his own part in this welled up in a spasm of furious anger. He jerked Rogan away, whirled him round, and sent him spinning across the room to land with a crash on the bed. 'I'm sorry, Father,' he said. 'Sorry for a lot of things. You can go now.'

For a moment he and the priest stood facing each other and a curious expression came into the old man's eyes. 'I'm sorry too,' he said. He hesitated in the doorway as if he was going to say something more and then his shoulders sagged and he went slowly out into the rain.

Fallon sighed deeply and a tiny, ironical laugh escaped from his mouth. The boy handed him his coat and hat. 'For God's sake, Mr Fallon, he'll put the peelers on us for sure. We've got to get out of here.' His face looked sickly and yellow under the naked bulb. He was frightened to death.

Rogan picked himself up from the bed and straightened his clothes. 'That was a fine thing to do,' he said. 'Now they'll know we're in town for sure.'

Fallon ignored him. 'Did you come in the car?' he asked Murphy.

The boy nodded. 'It's parked in the lane.'

Fallon pulled on his coat and said decisively. 'Right then! We'll have to make a run for it. If we can get out of town we might stand a chance yet. It's another filthy night. They'd have a job finding us in those country lanes.' He caught the boy by the shoulder and pushed him through the door. 'Come on, you,' he said over his shoulder to Rogan. 'We haven't any time to waste.'

He ran through the dripping gravestones after the boy. The door stood ajar in the wall and when he reached the car Murphy was already fumbling with the keys. He opened the door and scrambled behind the wheel and Fallon followed him into the front seat. The boy switched on the ignition and pressed the starter. The engine coughed protestingly, shuddered for a brief moment, and roared into life. 'Where's Rogan?' Murphy demanded and there was a crack in his voice.

Fallon swore violently and got out of the car and went back inside the graveyard.

As he stood fuming and peering through the gathering gloom Rogan appeared, running. 'Where the hell have you been?' Fallon snarled.

'I forgot something,' Rogan said breathlessly and Fallon pushed him towards the car and they scrambled in.

Murphy took the car away in a burst of speed and Fallon grasped him by the shoulder. 'Now steady down,' he said. 'We can't afford to attract any attention. Just take us through the town at a nice steady thirty miles an hour.'

The boy was sweating and Fallon lit a cigarette and pushed it between his lips. 'Thanks, Mr Fallon,' Murphy said. 'I'll be all right.'

'You're doing fine, son,' Fallon told him. He lit a cigarette himself and leaned back in the seat watching the road ahead of them.

'The kid's scared to death,' Rogan said. 'What good is he? We should drop him.'

Fallon turned and said deliberately, 'If I drop anyone it'll be you.' Rogan lapsed into silence and Fallon turned his eyes back to the road. He knew the hopelessness of their position. Already the town might be ringed with police. By the time they got the old priest's message they would have every road blocked with patrol cars. Their only chance was to beat the road blocks. Even as this thought flashed through his mind Murphy slowed down until they were crawling. There was a queue of cars in front of them, and Fallon realized with a sinking heart that they were too late.

'What shall I do, Mr Fallon?' Murphy said, and now his voice was steady and controlled.

'Cut into the next side street,' Fallon told him. 'We'll try the other road.' But he knew they were wasting their time.

The car twisted and turned through the back streets and came out into another main road. As they emerged from the turning Fallon saw another procession of vehicles in front of them and he tapped the boy on the shoulder and said, 'Turn right and go back to the centre of town.'

Rogan was cracking. There was panic in his voice. 'What are we going to do? We don't stand a chance.'

'Shut your mouth!' Fallon told him, and

at that moment he glanced into the mirror and saw the black car that was creeping up behind them. 'Get moving!' he screamed and Murphy rammed his foot down on the pedal and took the car away in a burst of speed.

'It's the polis,' Rogan said. 'We'll never beat a car like that.'

'They must have seen us turn away from that queue,' Fallon said. He watched the speedometer needle creep up to sixty and there it stopped.

'My foot's flat on the boards,' Murphy said desperately.

Fallon nodded and glanced back. The police car was pulling up on them. 'This is what we'll do. Change down and take the next turning on your right. Then take the first turning on the left, brake hard, and we'll jump out. Is that clear?'

The boy nodded vigorously and Rogan said, 'Pass me your gun and I'll try and catch their tyres.'

'No guns,' Fallon said. 'Only one of us has committed murder so far.'

Rogan's curse was drowned in the squeal

of brakes as Murphy changed down, braked, and skidded the car into the next turning. They were rushing along a dark side street lined with shabby terrace houses. Murphy switched on both headlights and they picked out the next turning when the car was still some way from it. He changed down again and braked. The car skidded broadside on and the wheels bumped across the corner of the pavement and then they were safe and rushing forward into the darkness. The lights picked up the entrance to a narrow alley. 'Now!' Fallon cried, clapping him on the shoulder. Murphy slammed his foot hard down on the brake and the car drifted at an angle and lurched against a lamp post with a sickening crunch.

For a moment there was silence. Somewhere a dog barked hollowly through the dark and Fallon wrenched open the door and jumped out. Murphy scrambled after him. 'You all right?' Fallon said.

The boy nodded. 'Bit of a bump, but it's nothing.'

Rogan joined them, cursing viciously. 'What a bloody mess,' he said.

'Bigger one if we stand here talking,' Fallon told him and at that moment the lights of the police car turned into the end of the street.

'Follow me,' Murphy said. 'I know this alley pretty well. We'll give them the slip yet.' He plunged into the alleyway and the others followed him.

Murphy twisted and turned through several back streets and alleys and after a while he stopped and held up his hand. 'What's wrong?' Fallon demanded.

'I'm trying to tell if they're following,' Murphy said.

Faintly in the darkness they could hear shouting and the noise of motor cars driving up. 'Christ, they're on to us now, all right,' Fallon said. 'Keep going.'

They commenced to run again and Murphy led the way as before. They cut across some waste ground where slum property was being demolished and ran into a long and narrow alley that seemed to go on for ever. Just before reaching the end Murphy called breathlessly over his shoulder, 'Watch it now. We're going to cross a busy street.' He slowed down to a jog-trot and turned the corner straight into the arms of a policeman.

As the constable fumbled for his revolver Murphy grappled with him and screamed, 'Run for it, Mr Fallon! Run for it!'

They went down in a mass of struggling limbs and Rogan cut straight across the road and disappeared down another side street. Fallon danced nimbly out of the way and as the constable rolled uppermost, he lifted his foot into the side of the man's neck. He subsided with a groan and Fallon jerked Murphy to his feet and dragged him across the road. The passers-by who had stopped to watch, quickly scattered, and Fallon and the boy plunged into the gloom of the side street.

As they neared the end of the street they saw Rogan standing under a lamp, poised for flight. 'I thought you were right behind me,' he said.

For a moment Fallon felt like smashing a fist into his face, but he resisted the impulse. 'Are you all right?' he said to Murphy.

'Yes, I'm fine,' the boy said. 'He didn't hurt me at all.'

Behind them a police whistle sounded faintly on the wind and a car turned into the end of the street. 'Where to now?' Fallon demanded.

'Follow close behind me,' Murphy said. 'There's just one chance left to us.'

He hurried along the street and darted into another alley. At the end of it was a low wall and when Fallon leaned over, he could hear the gurgle of water. Murphy lowered himself down and dropped into the water with a splash and Fallon and Rogan followed. The water was icy cold and knee-keep. Rogan cursed and Fallon told him sharply to be quiet. He touched the boy on the shoulder. 'We're ready,' he said and Murphy nodded and began to wade along the stream.

Brick walls towered on either side of them and once they had to go through a narrow tunnel that stretched for fifty or sixty yards. There was a pungent odour of decay and Fallon's nose wrinkled in disgust. He could guess what the stream was used for. They progressed in silence for about half an hour and all sounds of pursuit faded into the distance. There was only the rain hissing into the water and splashing as they moved on. Faintly in the distance there was the sound of traffic and then a church clock began to sound the hour. Murphy stopped. 'We'll climb up here,' he said.

It was not difficult. There were several bricks missing from the wall which was low at this point. There was a fence at the top with several gaps in it and they squeezed through one of them. They were in a quiet residential street. Murphy led the way along the pavement until they came to a little shop that stood on the corner. There was an entrance to one side that opened into a tiny yard and he turned into this and paused outside a door. 'Where are we?' Fallon said.

The boy smiled. 'My place.' Fallon started to protest and Murphy went on, 'There's nowhere else to go. We haven't any choice.'

From behind Rogan said, 'For God's sake let's go in if we're going,' and Murphy opened the door and walked into a tiny kitchen.

A young, pleasant-faced girl with a deter-mined face turned from the sink, her arms wet to the elbows. She picked up a towel and began to dry herself as she looked at them in amazement. 'Johnny!' she said. 'Where have you been?' Her eyes travelled down to their soaking legs that dripped water on to the floor.

Murphy cleared his throat nervously. 'We had a bit of an accident, Kathleen,' he said. 'These gentlemen are friends of mine.'

'Friends is it!' she said, interrupting him. She stepped forward and looked at Fallon closely and her expression altered and she paled. 'Dear God, you're Martin Fallon!' For a moment she swayed as though she would fall and then she seemed to regain her composure. She turned on her brother and said fiercely, 'What have you got yourself mixed up in now, you damned fool?'

'For God's sake, Kathy,' he said. 'Don't start arguing! We'll catch our deaths and the polis combing the streets for us. We'll have to stay here for the night.'

'Stay here is it?' she said, dangerously calm. 'If you think that, then you've another think coming. I'd rather they caught you now,

Johnny Murphy, before you get yourself more involved in this foolishness.' She turned and ran through into a small hall. A telephone stood on a table by the door. As she reached for the receiver, Rogan moved after her and caught her so roughly that the bodice of her dress ripped several inches.

'Leave her be, damn you!' Murphy screamed and threw himself at Rogan.

Fallon jumped between them and sent Rogan reeling against the wall. 'Stop it – both of you!' he shouted.

For the moment there was a lull and Fallon turned from Rogan's hate-filled eyes to the girl who was leaning over the table, weeping. 'I'm sorry, Miss Murphy,' he said. 'We won't trouble you any more.' He turned to the boy. 'You stay here with your sister.'

The girl choked back her sobs and said, 'That won't make any difference. I'm calling the police anyway, before he gets into this thing any deeper.'

She picked up the receiver and began to dial calmly and Fallon turned from her and went quickly out through the kitchen into the yard. He paused under the light outside and Rogan and the boy joined him. Fallon turned to argue, but Murphy shook his head. 'If you think I'm waiting here for the polis you're a damned fool, Mr Fallon. I'm sticking to you.'

Fallon laughed grimly. 'Much good it will do you now.'

The rain increased in volume and they started to walk along the street quickly. Rogan had the collar of his jacket turned up but it was an inadequate protection. He was soaked to the skin and cursing steadily. Suddenly Fallon felt desperate. The net was closing in and there was no place to run. No place to hide – but was that true? He paused abruptly and the boy said anxiously, 'Is anything the matter?'

Fallon shook his head slowly. 'I've just had an idea that's all. Do you know Cadogan Square?'

Murphy nodded. 'Surely, it's about half a mile from here.'

For a moment Fallon hesitated and then he made the decision. 'All right. Get us there as quickly as you can.'

Murphy nodded and stepped out briskly. He took to the back streets again, pausing at corners and cautiously checking for police before crossing the busier streets. It only took them twenty minutes to reach their destination. There were only three lamps lit and the far corners of the square were obscured by darkness. Fallon led the way across and when they reached the gate in the wall he hesitated for a moment. A sudden gust of wind drove rain in a fury into their faces, and he made his decision and opened the gate and led the way in.

He stood again on the top step and jerked on the ancient bell-pull. The force of the wind and rain was such that he couldn't hear the sound of the bell inside the house. They waited for a few moments and then a light came on in the hall. What on earth am I going to say to her? Fallon thought, and then the door opened and Anne Murray stood in a shaft of light peering out. For a brief moment she looked at him and then her gaze flickered to his two companions. He tried to speak and found that the words wouldn't come, and then she stood back and said, with a slight smile, 'Come in, Mr Fallon. I've been expecting you.'

5

It was chilly in the attic and the rain drummed relentlessly against a large glass skylight set in the sloping roof. In the centre of the room stood two rusty iron beds and piled in the corners were boxes containing the accumulated rubbish of years. Over everything there hung a faint musty smell of damp and decay. Rogan looked around with an expression of distaste. 'Is this the best she can do?'

Fallon laughed grimly. 'If you fancy going for another run round the back streets in the rain, you're welcome to go – on your own.'

Murphy came in, blankets piled high in his arms. 'It's fine by me, Mr Fallon,' he said. 'I've got a roof over my head and the polis are running round in circles in the rain. I know when I'm well off.'

Rogan snorted his disgust. 'You would,' he said. 'Quite the little yes-man, aren't you?'

Murphy flushed and tossed the blankets down on to one of the beds. 'At least I don't run off and leave people in the lurch,' he said. Rogan took a step towards him and the boy pushed half the blankets into his arms. 'There you are, Mr Rogan,' he said calmly. 'You can make your own bed at least.'

Rogan turned with a curse and dropped the blankets on to the bed. Fallon laughed and said, 'I think you'd better keep your lip buttoned, Rogan. You aren't too popular round here.' He moved forward until he stood very close to the small man. 'In fact it wouldn't take much to make me turn you out, and believe me that wouldn't be too healthy. The County Inspector only lives a couple of streets away. There must be quite a bit of police activity in this area.'

A peculiar expression showed in Rogan's eyes and then disappeared. He forced a laugh. 'Sure, I didn't mean anything. Dammit all, man, we're all living on our nerves at the moment.'

Fallon walked across to the door. 'Whatever happens,' he said, 'I don't want you to leave this room unless I tell you to.'

Murphy nodded obediently, but Rogan laughed, and there was a wealth of meaning in his voice. 'Where will you be sleeping then? She must have a fine sense of hospitality.'

For a moment violence sparked within Fallon, but as he took a step forward there was a movement behind him and the girl came into the room carrying a tray. She handed it to Murphy and said, 'There's a meal and hot coffee for you two. I don't want you prowling round the house, so stay in this room. If I have any trouble you can get out.' Her voice was cold and flat and completely unfriendly. She turned to Fallon. 'I've got a meal for you downstairs.' He nodded to his two companions and followed her out of the room.

It was warm in the kitchen. He sat down at the table and she spooned stew into a plate and set it before him. 'That smells good,' he said.

She laughed lightly. 'It's all I can make. I'm not very domestic, I'm afraid.'

He swallowed a mouthful of the warm food and shook his head. 'It's fine. Believe me, after what I've been through tonight, anything would be welcome.'

She smiled. 'That's rather a two-edged compliment, isn't it?'

He spread his hands in a gesture of humility. 'I'm sorry. I didn't mean it that way at all.'

He suddenly realized how hungry he really was and got down to the serious business of getting the food inside him. She watched him quietly for several minutes, not speaking, and when he had finished, brought him a cup of tea. As she poured milk into the cup she said, 'And how many dead men have you left behind you?'

He shook his head. 'Not a one, thank God. Did you expect that I would?'

She frowned and stirred her tea absently. 'No, it would be more true to say that I was afraid you would.' He stared at her in surprise, not understanding, and she explained. 'What

110

do you do when a policeman starts shooting at you? Don't you shoot back?'

He grinned. 'Personally I always run like hell.'

She sighed and nodded her head. 'But one day you *will* have to shoot back and that's what I'm afraid of.'

Fallon took out his cigarettes and offered her one. 'I hate the shooting side of it,' he said, as he held a match for her. 'Killing a policeman proves absolutely nothing, except perhaps that you're a good shot.'

'And what if you shoot them in the back at point blank range like Rogan did?' she said. 'What does that prove?'

His eyes narrowed. 'Who says he did that?'

She shrugged. 'That's how I heard it from Inspector Stuart. The one who was wounded told him. Rogan had them with their hands up. He told them to turn round and then shot them. The one who survived had his spine severed. He'll be in a wheelchair for life.'

He took the cigarette from his mouth and stubbed it carefully into the ashtray. 'All of a sudden everything tastes bad,' he said.

She shook her head impatiently and reached across and laid a hand on his sleeve. 'For God's sake, Martin, why did you get mixed up in this thing? Why?'

He stood up and moved a few paces away from the table. 'You asked me that yesterday,' he said. 'I couldn't give you a proper answer then and I can't now. One of the old leaders came to see me. He asked me to do this job and I laughed in his face, but then he produced Rogan's mother. She was a sort of trump card. He knew I wouldn't be able to turn her down.'

'I told you she wasn't a good enough reason,' Anne said.

He lifted his shoulders helplessly. 'I wish you could have seen her. Old and beaten down – and blind, as if enough hadn't happened to her. All she has left to hang on to is her son. I couldn't turn her down.'

'You mean you didn't have enough guts.'

He walked a few nervous paces and slammed a fist into the palm of his hand. 'All right. I didn't have enough guts. Have it any way you like.' He turned and looked at her despairingly for a moment and then he sat down and took one of her hands and gripped it strongly. 'Perhaps I was only looking for an excuse,' he said. 'I gave it all up because I wasn't convinced I was doing the right thing any more. I thought the Organization and everything it stood for was rotten. That's why I turned O'Hara down, and yet I gave in too quickly when the woman begged me to help her. Perhaps I was only looking for a good excuse.'

She nodded and there was something like understanding in her voice. 'There was something missing – something you couldn't find in that cottage. Did you think you'd find it back across the border?'

He frowned and sighed with exasperation and stood up again. 'I don't know. I really don't know.' He smiled sadly and moved across to the window and stared out into the driving rain and the night. When he spoke again it was slowly and from the very depths of his being. 'I lived by force for too many years.

Action and passion – they're funny things. Rather like drugs. When you've once tasted them anything else seems rather tame.'

She stood up wearily and began to clear the table. 'It's not enough,' she said. 'It never is enough. There must be something that can fill the hole in you.'

He turned from the window and smiled wistfully. 'I've looked for it for nearly five years,' he said. 'I thought I could be a great writer, but I'm only a third-rate hack. Then I tried the bottle, but that never solves anything.'

She looked across the length of the room at him. There was a terrible finality in her voice as she said, 'Whatever happens you'll have to find it soon. Without it you'll destroy yourself.'

He laughed sharply. 'Perhaps that's what I really want to do. Perhaps I really do want to be another martyr to the cause.'

A sob broke in her throat and she lifted a hand against her mouth and turned away. He crossed the room in three quick paces and pulled her close within his arms. For a few moments she sobbed bitterly, her head turned into his coat, and then she pulled herself away and forced a smile. 'There, you should be satisfied. You've made me make a fool of myself.'

He shook his head and said quietly, 'You could never be that.'

For a moment she smiled up at him and then she put a hand against his chest and pushed him away from her. 'Go on with you,' she said softly. 'Go to bed.' For a moment he stood there gazing at her searchingly and then he turned to the door. As he opened it she said sharply in something like her normal voice, 'You're in the room two doors past mine. Careful you don't make any mistakes if you're up during the night.'

A tiny smile tugged at the corners of his mouth. 'If I did,' he said, 'it would be the nicest mistake I ever made.' A crimson tide flooded her face and he closed the door quickly before she could make a reply.

As he moved along the hall to the foot of the stairs he suddenly realized that Rogan was bending over a small table that stood in the corner. For a moment Fallon watched him in silence and then he moved forward and said softly, 'I thought I told you to stay in your room?'

Rogan turned quickly, alarm on his face. He was holding a telephone directory in his hands and he replaced it on the table and laughed falsely. 'Sorry, Fallon. I was just checking up on the address of a friend.'

'Going visiting?' Fallon said sarcastically.

Rogan shook his head and started to climb the stairs. 'It was a fella I used to know in this town. I thought he might have been able to help us, but he isn't in the book any more. He must have moved.'

They mounted to the first floor and moved along the landing. At the bottom of the stairs that led to the attics they paused and Fallon said, 'Now this time try doing as you're told. Things are bad enough without you trying anything stupid.'

Rogan turned, fists clenched, and said bitterly, 'Don't push me too hard, Fallon. You may have been a big man once, but you've had your day.'

Fallon moved in close and crowded him

against the wall. 'Do you want a fight?' he said savagely. 'Because there's nothing I'd like better than to beat you to a pulp.' For a moment Rogan glared up at him and then he dropped his gaze. Fallon's voice became cold and deadly. It fell across Rogan like a whiplash. 'I saved your dirty hide because your mother begged me to. That's really funny because as far as I'm concerned she's better off without you. For the record I'd like you to know that you're just about the lowest rat I've ever come across.' For a moment longer he stood looking down at the small man and then he said quietly, 'Go on, get to bed.'

Rogan raised his head slowly and there was a terrible hate in his eyes. 'Good night to you, Mr Fallon,' he said, and turned and began to mount the stairs.

Fallon watched him until he was nearly at the top and then he said, 'And by the way, Rogan, I wouldn't advise you to try and shoot me in the back. You'd find it most unhealthy. In fact, I'm waiting hopefully for you to try.' Rogan paused on the top step without looking round and then continued up and disappeared into the gloom of the top landing.

As he got into bed Fallon checked his watch. It was only nine o'clock. The bed was cool and freshly made with clean linen sheets that smelt faintly of lavender. He guessed she must have unpacked them specially and smiled faintly in the darkness and sighed. He lit a cigarette and lay smoking and thinking about Anne Murray. She was something of a problem. He recalled the feel of her in his arms as she had cried against his shoulder and a wave of tenderness ran through him. For a moment or two he let his mind dwell on pleasant things. On how it might have been. He cursed softly and jerked his thoughts back to reality. It was pointless dwelling on what was now unattainable.

He tried to consider the problem rationally and logically. He desired the girl. And why not? She was attractive, young, almost beautiful, and he hadn't slept with a woman for longer than he cared to remember. But this wasn't the kind of girl one thought of just sleeping with. This girl would love one man, hard and fast, in every possible way she could. There was steel in her and integrity and even a fine touch of humour. What had she said? Don't make any mistakes if you're up during the night. He chuckled softly and turned over and went to sleep.

He came awake to a gentle, insistent pressure on one shoulder. His hand darted under the pillow and fastened over the butt of the Luger, and then he detected the elusive fragrance to which, by now, he was so well accustomed. He relaxed and sat up. 'Now who's picked on the wrong room?' he said.

'I'm sorry to bother you. It's silly, I know, but I thought I heard someone downstairs.' She sounded genuinely worried.

He pulled back the bedclothes and swung his feet to the floor. 'There's an easy way to find out,' he said. 'I'll go and check.'

Her nightdress rustled faintly through the darkness as she moved towards the door. 'I'll slip a dressing gown on and go with you,' she said.

He pulled on shirt and pants. For a moment he hesitated, weighing the Luger in his hand, and then he slipped it back under the pillow. He left the room quickly and found the girl waiting for him in the darkness by her door. Together they moved cautiously to the head of the stairs and listened. The house was as quiet as the grave. Fallon led the way down the back stairs and opened the door into the kitchen. The room was empty and quiet except for the faint crackling of the coke in the stove. He switched on the light and said, 'I'll check the other rooms, but it looks all right. Must have been the wind.'

When he came back she had the kettle boiling on the stove. 'Everything all right?' she said.

He grinned and looked at his watch. 'Well, it's now precisely ten minutes past six. Are you sure this wasn't just an excuse to get me up early?'

She smiled and shook her head. 'I really did think I heard something. It must have been my imagination. This old house is full of noises in the dark.'

Fallon lit a cigarette and sat down at the table as she poured tea. He coughed violently as the smoke caught at the back of his throat. 'Tastes horrible,' he managed to say at last.

She chuckled. 'Then why smoke?'

He shrugged and shook his head. 'Why do anything? Why live?'

She held up a hand and said, in mock alarm, 'Not philosophy. Not at this time in the morning, please.'

From the front of the house there came a faint rattling of bottles and Fallon turned quickly, every sense on the alert. 'What's that?' he demanded.

She smiled. 'Don't worry. It's only the milkman. They deliver very early here.' She got up from the table and went out into the hall.

Fallon heard her open the front door. There was the sound of heavy rain and the chink of the bottles as she picked them up, and then the door slammed. She came slowly into the room and he said, 'Hasn't it stopped yet?'

There was a puzzled expression in her eyes and she frowned as she put the bottles down on the table. 'I could have sworn I bolted that door,' she said.

'What was that?' He sat upright in his chair and looked at her.

'The door,' she said. 'I thought I bolted it last night.'

For a moment they stared at each other and then she paled and Fallon jumped to his feet, sending his chair flying and rushed out into the hall. He went up the stairs, two at a time, raced along the landing, and then up the flight that led to the attics. He flung open the door so that it crashed against the wall and switched on the light. Murphy sat up in bed, shocked from sleep, an expression of alarm and bewilderment on his face. 'For God's sake, Mr Fallon!' he cried. 'What's up?'

For a moment Fallon regarded the sleeping form of Rogan as he lay, huddled under the blankets, and then he took a quick pace forward and pulled the blankets away, disclosing two pillows. 'The bastard!' he said savagely. 'The crazy bastard! He'll be the end of all of us.' He turned to the boy. 'Get your clothes on and come down to the kitchen.' He turned on heel and left the room.

The girl was standing at the bottom of the stairs, an expression of alarm on her face. 'Is everything all right?' she said.

'Anything but,' Fallon told her. 'Rogan's gone for a walk.' He strode to the door and opened it and looked out into the darkness and the lashing rain.

'But why?' she said in amazement. 'I don't understand. Where could he go?'

Fallon shook his head and closed the door. 'I'd give a lot to know that,' he told her. 'All I know is that he's out there somewhere and there's a purpose in his going.' He turned and moved back towards the kitchen.

Murphy clattered down the stairs and rushed in. 'Have you any idea where's he's gone, Mr Fallon?' he said.

Fallon shook his head. 'Didn't you hear him get up?'

The boy flushed and looked at the floor. 'I was sleeping that sound I didn't hear a thing,' he said. 'I've let you down.'

Fallon snorted and clapped him on the

shoulders. 'Rubbish! You weren't supposed to be watching him, anyway.'

The girl handed Murphy a cup of tea. 'Did he say anything to you before you went to bed?' she said. 'Anything unusual, I mean?'

The boy frowned and shook his head. 'Nothing really unusual. He left the room for a while and I heard him arguing with Mr Fallon on the stairs. When he came in he was furious. He borrowed a pencil from me and wrote something on a piece of paper.'

Fallon looked up in interest. 'Did you see what he wrote? Was it an address?'

Murphy shook his head. 'I don't know, and that's a fact.'

Fallon explained to the girl. 'I caught him looking through the telephone directory. He said he was looking for the address of an old friend. He told me it wasn't in.' He turned to the boy. 'Anything else?'

Murphy shook his head. 'Nothing special. He made a few cracks about you before he went to sleep. Oh, and he raved on about the County Inspector. Said he'd make him sorry he'd ever been born.'

Fallon frowned and said in bewilderment, 'But why does he hate Phil Stuart so much?'

Anne smiled bitterly. 'Because he did a good job. Because he chased Rogan into the ground, didn't give him a moment's peace for two months until he had him by the heels.'

Murphy nodded in agreement. 'It's his pride you know, Mr Fallon,' he said. 'He's a terrible man to cross. They say he never forgives anyone who does him an injury.'

Fallon cursed and kicked the table savagely. 'It was a black day for me when I first heard his name.'

'Shall we go after him, Mr Fallon?' Murphy suggested.

Fallon laughed coldly. 'After him? Where's he gone? Do you know? I'm damned if I do.' He shrugged his shoulders and moved towards the door. 'No, all we can do is wait. If he's skipped out thinking he's a better chance on his own, then he won't be back and we're well rid of him. If he's gone to see somebody, then he'll be back in his own sweet time. Unless the police pick him up,' he added grimly.

'But what if the peelers do pick him up?' the boy said. 'I don't trust him. He's yellow, Mr Fallon. He'd be likely to sick them onto us.'

Fallon smiled sourly. 'I know,' he said. 'That's a chance we'll have to take.' He turned to go, hesitated and said slowly to Murphy, 'I think you'd better keep a watch from the front room. At the slightest sign of movement give me a yell. We'll make a run for it through the back garden. I'll be in the bathroom if you want me.'

He filled the wash basin with cold water and plunged his head into it several times. Then he turned on the hot tap and washed his face and shoulders thoroughly. He found a razor in the bathroom cabinet and the blade was still in reasonable condition. He lathered his face with soap and attacked the thick bristles of his beard. He thought about Rogan and wondered what the small man was up to. He felt uneasy. There was something rotten about Rogan, something unhealthy. The man wasn't normal. Fallon patted his face dry and pulled his shirt over his head. He sighed.

What a mess. What a bloody mess. He regarded himself in the mirror and shook his head. 'You never learn,' he said softly. 'You never learn.'

He moved along the landing and started to descend the stairs and suddenly the girl screamed from the kitchen, high and long. It was a cry of pure agony. For a split second Fallon froze there and then he leapt down the stairs into the hall and turned towards the kitchen. Murphy emerged from the front room, an expression of alarm on his face. 'My God!' he cried, 'what is it?'

Fallon didn't even try to answer. He moved fast to the kitchen door and wrenched it open. Anne Murray was huddled over the table, her body shaking with sobs. Fallon glanced widly around. There was no intruder. The radio was on, a neutral voice announced the end of the news at that moment, and he moved across and switched it off. He bent over the girl and placed a hand on her shoulder. 'Anne,' he said. 'What is it? What happened?'

Slowly she turned her head and looked up at him. Tears stained her cheeks and there was an expression of loathing on her face. 'It was the news,' she said brokenly. 'The seven o'clock news. You were hiding in the vaults at St Nicholas yesterday, weren't you? Father Maguire found you. He told you to get out and went for the police.' Fallon nodded dumbly, a terrible unease tugging at his heart, and she went on, 'The police went to the vaults last night. A young constable opened the door. Someone had fastened a hand grenade to it with string. It blew up in his face.' Fallon stared down at her in horror and she stood up and pushed her face right into his. 'He's dead,' she screamed. 'He was twenty-one years of age and you killed him.'

Fallon shook his head. His mind was numb. He could only remember one thing clearly – Rogan's unaccountable delay in following them to the car when they left the vault. He moistened his lips and managed to speak. 'It was Rogan,' he said, 'Rogan did it.'

She shook her head. Her whole body was broken with her weeping. 'It was you,' she said. 'You set him free. You turned him loose to prey on decent people.'

Fallon turned away blindly, and Murphy reached out and touched him with shaking fingers. 'It wasn't our fault, Mr Fallon, was it?' There was a note of utter despair and horror in his young voice.

Fallon tried to speak and found there was nothing to say. There was no answer and then the front door bell rang. There was a moment of stillness as the three of them looked at each other and the girl checked her sobbing and stood, a hand at her mouth, eyes wide and shining with fear. Murphy went quickly along the hall and peered out through the side window as the bell sounded insistently again. He took a few paces back towards them, his face white and strained, and said quietly, 'It's Rogan.'

Fallon hesitated for a moment and then walked forward very slowly. 'Open the door and let him in,' he breathed.

The bell sounded again as Murphy opened the door. There was a brief glimpse of the silver rain lancing down through the grey morning and then Rogan banged the door shut and collapsed against it, breathless and laughing. He gulped for breath and said, 'I nearly had it then. A peeler stopped me a couple of streets away. I gave him a kick and ran like hell.' He laughed unsteadily and pushed back a lock of wet hair from his forehead. The smile died on his face at the terrible silence which greeted him. His gaze passed from Murphy to the girl and then to Fallon. He licked his lips nervously. 'You lot look cheerful, I must say.'

'Where have you been?' Fallon said calmly.

Rogan managed a smile. 'That friend I told you about. I thought I'd see if he was still at his old address. I thought maybe he'd had the phone taken out.'

Fallon lashed him back-handed across the face. 'You bloody liar,' he said. 'Where have you been?'

'Murderer!' Anne Murray screamed. 'You filthy murderer.'

Panic moved across Rogan's face and he turned, one hand reaching for the door-knob, but Fallon beat him to it. He swung him round and held him by the jacket and he slapped him repeatedly across the face with the flat of his hand. 'You fixed that grenade up at the church, didn't you?' he shouted. 'You knew it would blow up in the face of the first person to open the door.'

Rogan's eyes had dwindled into pinpricks. He stared into Fallon's implacable face and a thin line of foam appeared on the edge of his lips. Fallon gave an exclamation of disgust and pushed him hard against the door. As Rogan slumped back something fell from inside his coat. Fallon bent down quickly and picked it up. It was one of the belts of plastic gelignite that had been in the second box in the vault. For a moment he stared at it in horror. Two pockets were empty. He moved towards Rogan and held the belt under his nose. 'You fixed up that grenade and killed one man. Now you've been up to your tricks again. Where have you been?' He smashed Rogan back-handed with the belt of explosive and Rogan screamed with rage and threw himself on Fallon, sending him reeling back against the foot of the stairs.

The small man leaned against the door, eyes staring, foam dribbling from his mouth.

'Yes, I fixed that grenade up,' he screamed. 'I fixed it up because I hoped it might kill somebody. That's what I'm here for. To kill people. That's what the Organization needs.' He seemed to choke for a second and then he recovered and pointed a quivering finger at Fallon. 'It doesn't need men like you – frightened to spill a little blood, worried about your drivelling consciences.' He began to laugh, tears streaming down his face.

'God help us, he's mad, Mr Fallon,' Murphy said in a terrified voice.

Rogan straightened up. 'Mad is it?' he snarled. 'It takes a madman to get things done then. While you clever ones slept I was out in the rain and the dark looking for an address. An address just three streets away. And I found it. I spent half an hour underneath Mr God-Almighty Stuart's car. Just half an hour.' He cackled and wiped the spittle from his chin with the back of his hand. 'They'll be needing a new County Inspector before the morning's out.'

Anne Murray lifted a hand to her mouth and stifled a scream. 'Martin!' she wailed.

Fallon stood as if turned to stone and Rogan suddenly lashed out with one foot that connected with Murphy's shins. He whirled round, wrenched open the door and ran out into the rain. They had a final glimpse of him as he bounded down the path and then the door in the wall banged and he was gone.

Murphy was doubled up against the wall, clutching his right knee. Fallon turned to him quickly. 'Are you all right?' he said.

The boy nodded. 'The bastard caught me on the knee-cap.'

Anne caught hold of Fallon's arm and turned him round. 'What's he done to Philip Stuart? What did he mean?'

Fallon lifted up the belt of explosive. 'From the sound of it he's put a sort of time bomb under Stuart's car. It's a trick from the last war. You fasten a lump of plastic gelignite to the underneath of the car and attach the fuse to the exhaust pipe with insulating tape. When the car's been driven for five minutes or so the pipe gets hot enough to ignite the fuse.'

An expression of horror came into her eyes. 'Martin, you've got to save him.'

He nodded reassuringly and took her by the shoulders. 'I intend to. Don't worry. It's unlikely he'll be using the car for a while yet.'

She shook her head obstinately. 'That's not true. When there's trouble he's out at all hours. That's why men like Rogan fear him so much. He never stops, never lets up. He was out at five yesterday morning.'

Fallon nodded. 'Perhaps you're right. I'll phone him right away.'

He turned to lift the receiver and she cried, 'But the phone isn't working. I asked them to cut it off because I was leaving.'

For a brief moment they stood staring at each other and Fallon felt his flesh turn cold. It was as though a grey wave ran through him, lifting the hair on the back of his head, and he was afraid. More afraid than he had ever been. 'What's the address?' he said urgently.

'The street in the far corner of the square,' she said. 'It's the third turning along on the left. A tall, narrow house, with a basement garage painted blue. Number four.'

He gripped her arms firmly and said, 'I

want you to stay here. Keep the boy with you. Whatever happens don't let him follow me.' She nodded dumbly, and unexpectedly he smiled. 'They told me this was going to be a desperate bloody business,' he said and turned and ran down the garden path, out through the open door into the square.

He ran very fast and before he had gone far the heavy rain had soaked his shirt, wetting him to the skin, running down from his hair into his eyes. He turned into the street in the corner of the square and splashed through a swollen gutter. There was no one about and he ran on alone along the empty pavement, never stopping even when a foot slipped and he almost lost his balance. As he approached the third street, a saloon car emerged from the turning and proceeded along the road in the direction in which he was running. He turned into the street and searched for number four. The blue garage doors were there as she had described, but they were standing open and the car had gone.

For a moment Fallon hesitated and then he ran up the steps and hammered at the front door. He kept on banging until it was opened. A woman in a housecoat stood in the doorway. He didn't give her a chance to speak. 'How long has Inspector Stuart been gone?' he said.

'Why, he's just left this minute,' she said. 'I'm Mrs Stuart. Is there anything I can do?'

He raised a hand wearily and pushed hair away from his eyes. 'I've got to get to him,' he said. 'It's a matter of life and death. Was he in the black saloon that passed me at the end of the street?'

'That's right,' she said. 'He's gone to the newsagents along the road for the morning paper. He'll be back for breakfast before he leaves.' And then her eyes widened and her voice changed. 'You're Martin Fallon.'

He turned without answering and ran down the steps along the path out into the street. He turned the corner and stared into the grey morning, but there was no sign of Stuart returning. He began to run along the pavement, his lungs labouring for breath, his feet slipping on the wet flagstones. He was thinking of Philip Stuart driving his car casually along in the quiet morning, while underneath him his exhaust pipe grew steadily hotter. Five minutes, Fallon thought, that's all it takes. He stumbled and fell flat on his face, grazing his right arm badly. For a moment he lay there and then he pushed himself to his feet and ran on. Jesus Christ, what a bloody mess! he thought, and then he saw the black saloon coming towards him out of the rain.

He staggered into the road, arms outstretched and the car skidded to a halt a bare two feet away from him. He caught a glimpse of Stuart's startled face through the windscreen and then he was alongside the car, wrenching open the door and grabbing at him. 'Martin!' Stuart cried in amazement. 'What the hell are you doing here?'

Fallon dragged him bodily out of the car so that he slipped and fell into the road on his knees. 'Bomb!' he managed to gasp as his lungs fought for air. 'Bomb under car. Let's get out of here.'

He turned and ran for the far side of the road, Stuart at his heels, and then there was a tremendous explosion and out of the corner of his eye, he saw a large piece of metal flying through the air. He flung himself face down on the pavement and huddled there, his head buried in his arms. As the echoes of the explosion died flatly away on the morning air, there was a tremendous rushing sound and a further small explosion as the petrol went up.

He lifted his head and breathed deeply. Stuart was lying slightly behind him. Fallon got to his knees and said, 'You all right, Phil?'

Stuart struggled to one knee. There was an expression of bewilderment on his face. 'Martin,' he said. 'I don't understand. What's going on?'

Fallon opened his mouth to answer him and then there was the roar of engines and two patrol cars came along the street fast and skidded to a halt with a squeal of brakes. Fallon laughed bitterly. Mrs Stuart hadn't wasted any time. 'Tell your wife she did a good job,' he said hastily to the astonished Stuart and started to run along the pavement.

He cut diagonally across the road, dodged past one car and took to his heels. He had only gone a few yards when another car turned out of a side street in front of him and slewed across the road. Behind him Stuart called, loud and clear, 'Martin, don't be a fool!'

Fallon slowed as three constables piled out of the car in front and came towards him. Despair and a furious anger rose in his throat. Before him on the pavement there was a twisted piece of metal from the car. It was the only available weapon. He picked it up and turned and ran, crouching, back towards Stuart and the other two cars. He heard a voice shout, 'Look out! He's got a gun!' and then Stuart's terrible cry, 'No – don't shoot!'

That was the last thing he heard because there was the sudden, flat report of a revolver and something kicked him violently in the chest. He was lying on the pavement, his head pillowed against the wet flagstones, and there was a confused murmur of voices and a forest of legs surrounding him. A face came close to his and a voice sounded from a very long way off, and then the face disappeared into a whirlpool of coloured lights and he plunged into darkness.

6

There was a light that came very close and went away again. It did this several times. Fallon found it extremely irritating. His head was spinning and it was an effort to open his eyes. The light came very close again and this time there was a voice saying: 'Relax! Don't struggle. Just relax.' The light suddenly dwindled into a spinning ball that got smaller and smaller and he was in darkness again.

When he finally awoke he found himself in a single bed. The room was small and narrow and over everything there was that peculiar and distinctive hospital smell of disinfectant and cleanliness.

The room was half in shadow and there was a shaded lamp on a locker beside the bed. A young nurse was reading in the light of the lamp. Fallon tried to push himself up and groaned. It felt as if there was an iron band around his chest. The nurse looked up quickly and put down her book. She stood up and moved across to the door and opened it. 'Will you call for Doctor Flynn, please?' she said to some anonymous person in the corridor and closed the door again. She came over to the bed.

Fallon grinned weakly. 'So I'm still in the land of the living?' he said. 'Life's full of surprises.'

She put a hand on his brow. It was cool and sweet and he closed his eyes. 'Just rest,' she said. 'You shouldn't even talk.'

The door opened and he lifted his eyelids. He saw a brown, kindly face, seamed with wrinkles and topped with iron-grey hair. His wrist was lifted delicately and the doctor looked at his watch and said, 'How do you feel?'

'Lousy!' Fallon told him.

The doctor smiled. 'You're the lucky one. The bullet was turned by your ribs. It's a nasty wound but you won't peg out on us yet awhile.'

Fallon raised his eyebrows. 'And you call that lucky?'

The doctor shrugged and laughed lightly. 'All I do is patch 'em up,' he said. 'What they do with them afterwards isn't my affair.'

There was a discreet knock on the door. The nurse opened it and said, 'Oh, Doctor. Inspector Stuart is here.'

The doctor turned to the door as Philip Stuart entered. 'You can have fifteen minutes,' he said. 'No longer. He needs plenty of sleep.' He smiled at Fallon. 'I'll see you in the morning.' He went out followed by the nurse.

Stuart moved out of the shadows and smiled down. He was tall and lithe and his uniform fitted him like a glove. 'Hello, Martin,' he said. 'How do you feel?'

Fallon grinned weakly. 'Like a cigarette. Have you got one?'

Stuart nodded. He pulled a chair forward and sat down and then he took out a cigarette case. Fallon inhaled deeply and sighed with pleasure. 'That's better,' he said.

'I'm sorry about this,' Stuart said. 'One of my young constables panicked. When you turned with that bit of metal in your hand he thought you'd drawn a gun.'

Fallon nodded. 'That's all right, Phil. I heard your shout just before the bullet hit me. It doesn't seem to have done much damage.' He laughed lightly. 'What about your car? Is any of it left?'

Stuart shrugged. 'It might fetch a few pounds for scrap.'

'I'm sorry about that,' Fallon sighed. 'It was a good job I got to you as fast as I did.'

'Was it Rogan?' Stuart said.

Fallon nodded. 'Yes, it was Rogan.'

'And the booby trap at the church? Was that Rogan, too?'

Fallon stubbed out his cigarette in the ashtray on the bedside locker. He lay back against the pillows. 'I'm sorry about that,' he said. 'I didn't know anything about it until I heard the news this morning.'

Stuart jumped up in disgust. 'He's a mad dog,' he said forcefully. He moved restlessly about the room. 'If there was ever a man I wanted to lay by the heels it's Patrick Rogan. I want to see him hang.'

Fallon said quietly, 'Yes, he's about the worst I've come across. If I'd had any sense I'd have killed him myself. It would have saved a lot of grief.'

'Instead you set him free,' Stuart said.

Fallon nodded slowly. 'That's right. I set him free. That makes me responsible for anything he does, I suppose?'

Stuart stood at the end of the bed, his face darkened by a line of shadow. 'Why did you leave that cottage of yours, Martin?'

Fallon looked at him in amazement. 'You knew where I was?'

Stuart nodded. 'I've often stood at the border post at Doone and looked at your cottage through field glasses.' He laughed suddenly. 'My God, what did you expect? Did you think we'd lose all interest in

Martin Fallon once he was out of our hands? We expected you back long ago.' He moved back to his chair and sat down. 'Personally, I was glad when you didn't come back.'

Fallon smiled. 'I wish to hell I never had,' he said feelingly.

'Why did you?' Stuart demanded. 'What made you come back after five years to help a mad dog who's only fit for the gallows?'

Fallon shook his head. 'Now don't you start,' he said. 'I'm getting rather tired of that question. The only important thing is that I did come and I've made a proper muck-up of everything.' He laughed bitterly. 'Do you realize I still have six years to serve from my last sentence? How much do you think I'll get this time?' Stuart's face darkened. He got up and walked across to the window and stood looking out into the darkness without saying anything. There was a silence and after a while Fallon sighed. 'Come on, Phil. Tell me the worst. What will I get?'

Stuart turned slowly. For the moment he

was the policeman again, calm-voiced, dry, matter-of-fact. 'I'm afraid you're an accessory to murder this time,' he said.

Fallon nodded slowly. 'And for that they could hang me,' he said.

'Very possibly.' Stuart moved back to the bed and said, gently, 'Of course, the fact that you saved my life will help you a lot.' He hesitated and went on, 'And any useful information you give us would have a definite effect on the outcome of your trial.'

'Such as Rogan's whereabouts?' Fallon enquired.

Stuart nodded. 'And where you've been hiding out since leaving the church.' He frowned. 'I thought I'd rooted out the Organization in Castlemore.'

Fallon smiled slightly. 'I can answer the first part of your question very easily. I haven't the slightest idea where Rogan is. As to where I've been hiding – you can find that out for yourself.'

Stuart pursed his lips and frowned again. 'You were in your shirt sleeves when you came looking for me,' he said, 'so you couldn't have been very far away from my house.'

Fallon settled his head comfortably against the pillow. 'Good night, Phil,' he said.

Stuart picked up his cap and set it on his head, pulling the peak slightly over his eyes. When he spoke his voice was quite cold. 'You're on the second storey of this hospital,' he said. 'I've got a twenty-four-hour guard on the door. Don't try anything foolish.'

'I couldn't even walk to the toilet,' Fallon told him.

Stuart turned to the door. He paused for a moment, his hand on the door knob, and said very quietly, 'My wife sends her thanks, Martin, for what you did.' His voice seemed to crack and he swallowed and went on, 'We're expecting a child next month, so . . .' His voice trailed off.

'That's all right, Phil,' Fallon said softly.

Stuart coughed. 'She wanted me to tell you that she'll be praying for you.' For a moment longer he stood there in the shadows and then the door closed quietly behind him.

Praying for me, Fallon thought. A lot of good that's going to do me. He stared up at the ceiling and beads of sweat formed on his brow. Accessory to murder. The words seemed to flame out of the shadows at him. By some trick of memory he recalled his dream of being on the train in Rogan's place and he shuddered. The judge had worn the black cap. Perhaps it was prophetic.

He wondered what Anne Murray was thinking about now. The circumstances surrounding his capture would have made front page news all over the province. She'd know where he was. He frowned as he thought of Murphy and hoped fervently that she would stop the boy from doing anything silly.

He began to think of her, calmly and deliberately, letting his mind dwell on each separate incident. There were so many things to think about. Why had she given them sanctuary? – but the answer to that was so simple and he had been pushing it away from him deliberately because he hadn't wished to acknowledge the fact.

All at once he knew that he didn't want to die. He wanted to see Anne Murray again with a sudden fierce desire that had him struggling to sit up in the bed. Sweat broke out on his forehead and his senses reeled. He closed his eyes and hung on and when he opened them again it was all right. He pushed back the bedclothes and swung his feet to the floor. His chest was tightly swathed in bandages and there was a dull, throbbing pain in his left side. He took a deep breath and got to his feet. For a moment he stood swaying there, and then he began to walk.

He felt curiously light-headed and for a few moments it was as if he was walking on cotton wool and then he reached the far wall. He rested for a while then turned and walked back. He sat on the edge of the bed and then tried again. There was a cupboard in one corner. He opened it hopefully but was disappointed. His clothes weren't there. He moved over to the window and looked cautiously out, keeping behind the curtain. When his eyes became accustomed to the darkness he saw that the ground was some forty feet below. His heart sank and he turned and staggered back to his bed. He had barely got himself settled again when the door opened and the nurse came in.

She punched his pillows and smoothed the blankets into place. 'How do you feel?' she said.

He groaned a little and answered her in a weak voice, 'Not so good. I think I'll go back to sleep.'

She nodded and compassion showed in her eyes. 'I'll look in later on. Try and get some rest.' She left the room as quietly as she had come.

Fallon smiled softly. So far so good. He pulled back the bedclothes and moved across to the door. There was a murmur of conversation outside and the nurse laughed. He placed his head close against the door and heard her say, 'You'll be bored to death sitting here all night.'

A man's voice replied, 'Not if I had something as pretty as you to keep me company.'

She laughed again. 'You read your book,' she said. 'I'll be round at half-past eleven to have a look at him. I'll bring you a cup of tea.' Her heels clicked away along the corridor and Fallon heard the creaking of a chair as the policeman settled into it.

He moved unsteadily back towards the bed. There was an electric clock on the wall and it showed the time as nine-thirty. He walked across the room two or three times and sat down again. He had an hour and a half. It was like the train affair all over again. He had only one chance – surprise. He had to move fast. If he didn't get away now he knew that he never would. Tonight was the one slack period. The time when they thought him so ill and shocked that the very thought of escape was laughable.

He checked the bedside locker. There was nothing there except some towels and a pair of slippers. He pulled the slippers on and turned out the light, then he moved across to the window.

Slightly to the right and about thirty feet below there was a side entrance to the hospital. A lamp jutted out from the wall on an iron bracket casting a pool of light down on to the path. A fine rain drifted through the yellow light like silver mist. He opened the window carefully and leaned out.

About three feet below the window-sill an ornamental stone ledge about six inches wide, cut across the face of the building. A sudden excitement moved inside him. To the right, a line of windows stretched away into the darkness, almost every one throwing a broad shaft of light into the darkness. To his left there were three windows and only the middle one showed a light.

Fallon hardly paused to consider the problem. There was no risk involved because his life was in far greater danger if he stayed. He threw a leg over the sill and clambered out on to the ledge. For a moment he stood holding on to the comparative safety of the open window and then he began to move cautiously along the ledge, step by step, his face to the wall.

He wasn't conscious of the cold or of the

wind cutting through the thin material of his pyjamas. He moved inch by inch, his mind fiercely concentrated on maintaining his balance on the narrow ledge. It seemed an age before he reached the first window. It was open several inches at the bottom. He slid his fingers into the slight gap and lifted the sash and climbed in. He moved across the room carefully, straining his eyes through the darkness, but the bed was unoccupied. He walked quickly to the door and turning the knob gently, opened it a couple of inches. Just a few feet away a police sergeant was sitting in a chair reading a book. Fallon quietly closed the door.

He wasted no time. He padded back across the dark room and clambered out on to the ledge again. It seemed colder this time and he shivered as he began to move along towards the next window. He was lucky. The light that showed escaped through a slight gap in drawn curtains and he paused to rest for only a second or two before moving on towards the last window. It was slightly further away than the others had been and when he reached it his arms were trembling.

His fingers scrabbled for a moment at the window frame and panic moved in him when the window remained closed. He pushed again, straining every finger, and the window shot up with a clatter and he lost his balance and half fell across the sill. Pain knifed into his ribs and he stifled a cry of agony and scrambled into the room. For a moment he sat on the floor waiting for the pain to pass. After a time, when it was simply a dull ache, he got to his feet and went cautiously forward. His head bumped into a wall and he moved along it until he reached the door. He turned the knob gently and pulled. Nothing happened. For a moment he stood motionless, breathing heavily, and then he ran his hands over the wall at the side of the door until they encountered the light switch.

He was in a linen room. The walls were lined with wooden shelves that were piled high with sheets and blankets and towels. He tried the door again. It was no use.

He switched off the light and went and stood by the open window. There was no despair in his heart but he was worried. He'd over-taxed his strength already. If he passed out now he wouldn't stand a chance. He'd never get away. He remembered again Stuart's words and a sudden new energy flooded through him. He climbed out on to the ledge and started back towards his own room.

It seemed to take twice as long on the return journey and once he almost lost his balance and fell. It was only by a miracle he managed to retain his footing. At last he pulled himself over the sill, back into his own room, and staggered across to the bed and sat down. He didn't feel so good. He was breathing with difficulty because his chest seemed to be constricted by the bandages. He considered the position. It was no use trying the ledge along to the right. There was a light on in almost every room. Someone was bound to see him. It was even possible that those were the windows of a ward. No, he would have to think of something else.

He looked at the clock. It was ten-fifteen. He whistled softly to himself. It must have taken longer to get along that ledge than he had imagined at the time. He moved back to the window and leaned out again. There was no way out above him. The eaves of the roof were several feet out of reach. The next row of windows was some ten feet below. He leaned far out and looked down. There was no light in the room directly beneath him.

He hardly considered the danger involved as he stripped his bed quickly and knotted the two sheets and the bedspread together. Underneath the window-sill ran the iron pipe of the central heating system and he carefully tied one end of his improvised rope round it and threw the other out over the window-sill. He clambered out and stood on the ledge and took a firm grip on the sheets and began to slide down. A terrible pain like fire coursed through his chest and side and for a moment his senses swam so that he almost lost his grip, and then his feet bumped against the window-sill of the room below and he was safe. He swayed there for a moment, hanging on to his lifeline grimly and then he reached out with a trembling hand and attempted to open the window. It was locked. He lifted his elbow recklessly and pushed it hard against the glass. A sudden gust of wind whirled round the corner of the building and half-drowned the sound of breaking glass. He reached in through the jagged hole and unfastened the catch. A second later he was crouching in the warm darkness, sobbing for breath.

There was no time to waste. He walked forward, arms outstretched, until he touched the wall, then he moved along until his fingers encountered a light switch. He was in another private room. Blankets were piled neatly in a squared tier on the bed and the room was obviously unoccupied. The door opened at a touch and he sighed with relief and looked out on to a deserted corridor. He closed the door and began to make a rapid search of the room. In the wardrobe he found a faded blue hospital dressing gown and he pulled it on. He turned out the light and left the room.

He walked slowly along the corridor, his senses alert for danger. What his next move was to be he did not know. He preferred to leave it to chance. He felt calm and fatalistic now because, in some queer way, he knew that he was going to get away with it. As he came to the end of the corridor he heard voices talking quietly. He peered round the corner. A few feet away from him two police constables leaned against the banisters at the stairhead. They were both armed with automatic rifles.

Stuart was obviously taking no chances. Fallon retraced his steps. When he reached the opposite end of the corridor he drew back hastily. A police constable was standing with his back to him only four or five feet away.

Fallon considered the situation for a moment. The fact that the corridors and stairs were so heavily guarded meant that all entrances and exits must be heavily guarded as well. Sweat was oozing from his forehead in bright drops. He brushed it away with his hand. At any moment someone might appear in the corridor and there was his improvised rope of sheets still hanging out of the window. It only needed a passer-by to glance upwards. As he paused, his brain racing, he noticed a small door about three feet square, set in the opposite wall of the corridor, rather like a window. He moved across quickly and opened it. He looked down into the depths of a lift shaft.

He began to heave on the ropes feverishly and within a few seconds the lift appeared. In it there was a wicker basket full of dirty sheets and towels. He dragged out the basket hastily and scrambled into the lift. It was a tight squeeze and he was doubled over so that his face almost rested on his knees. The strain on his wound was almost unbearable and it felt as though the bandages were cutting into his flesh. He closed the door and pulling quickly on the ropes, dropped jerkily down into the darkness.

He passed through several rays of light which found their way through lower entrances into the lift shaft. He kept on going down without stopping, until he bumped against the concrete base of the shaft. He opened the small door cautiously and scrambled out. He was in a large basement room that was brightly lit by three naked electric bulbs. The room was filled with piles of dirty sheets and blankets tied together in bundles. There seemed to be no one about. He moved across to the far door and opened it.

He found himself in a long, whitewashed corridor. He began to walk quickly along it, checking the rooms as he did so. He heard voices coming from a door at the far end. It was slightly open and he peered in. Two men in overalls were standing by several large boilers, leaning on their shovels and laughing over some joke. He passed on and turned the corner into a smaller corridor in which there were just two doors. He opened the first one and found himself in a lavatory. The other room seemed to be some sort of rest room. There was a table and two benches and a couple of battered tin lockers stood against one wall. He moved across quickly and opened them. One of them contained only a few odds and ends of personal belongings. In the other, he found a pair of broken, steel-tipped industrial boots and an old, shabby jacket. He took them out quickly and then, as he turned, his eyes lighted on a boiler suit hanging behind the door on a hook. It was the work of a few seconds to take off his dressing gown and pull the boiler suit over his pyjamas. He sat down and laced on the heavy boots. He stood up and pushed his arms into the sleeves of the jacket and at that moment the door opened and a man walked in.

It was one of the men Fallon had seen in the boiler room. His mouth went slack in amazement and then a sudden anger sparked in his eyes as he noticed the jacket Fallon was pulling on. 'Here, that's my jacket,' he said. He clenched his fists menacingly. 'What the hell do you think you're doing?'

Fallon didn't waste any time in arguing. He was in no condition to fight fairly. There was an old, broken chair leaning against the wall behind him. He snatched it up and smashed it down across the head and shoulders of the unfortunate intruder. The man sank to his kees with a terrible groan. He tried to get up, his arms reaching out as Fallon moved for the door. His grasping fingers tore at the jacket and Fallen turned and kicked him in the stomach. The man went over backwards and writhed on the floor, his face slowly turning purple.

Fallon moved quickly along the corridor. As he drew abreast of the boiler room the other man came running out, drawn by the sounds of conflict. They smashed into each other and Fallon called out as pain flooded the upper half of his body. The man grabbed at him with huge, work-hardened hands and Fallon lifted his knee up hard into his crutch. As the man subsided on to the floor like a deflated balloon, Fallon ran on and quickly mounted the steps at the end of the corridor.

The pain moved in him like a living thing, but he pushed it deliberately away from him, opened the door, and walked calmly out. He was in a narrow corridor that opened into a small hall. There was a tiny glass office in the hall by the entrance and two police constables were sitting in it drinking tea. The glass entrance doors were standing open and outside he could see a loading ramp. A large van was standing against the ramp with its tailboard down and piled in the back were several skips. The corridor seemed to be full of similar skips. Fallon moved forward and grabbed one by the handle, then he began to pull it across the hall. He was sweating with fear and his heart was in his mouth. As he passed the glass office he didn't look up. He waited for the sudden shout but it never came. He pulled the skip into the van and stood there for a moment thinking and then he came to a sudden decision. He stepped out on to the ramp and lifted the tailboard, hooked it into position. He dropped off the ramp, walked along the side of the van, and climbed up into the cab. The engine roared into life at the first touch of the accelerator. He released the handbrake and drove slowly away.

Again he waited for the sound to come from behind. For the sudden cries of alarm, but all was quiet. He turned into the drive and approached the main gates. There were two policemen on guard, sub-machine guns crooked in their arms. He slowed to stop but one of them raised an arm and waved him on. He turned into the main road and drove quietly away.

He took the van into the centre of Castlemore and parked it in the main street within three or four minutes of leaving the hospital. The rain was still drifting softly down and it was cold and raw. He shivered and lifted the collar of the old jacket up around his neck and began to walk rapidly through the side streets. Strangely enough he felt no particular jubilation. He was tired, very tired, and curiously light-headed. He felt almost sorry for Philip Stuart. It was as though he had played a rather dirty trick on him. Friends shouldn't do that sort of thing to each other.

He staggered suddenly and lurched into a

lamp post and clung to it desperately. What nonsense was he thinking of now? What was happening to him? He looked up at the lamp above him and suddenly it seemed to dim. He closed his eyes and re-opened them and it brightened again. He started to walk faster. It wouldn't do to collapse in the street. That would be stupid.

It was with a sense of surprise that he found himself crossing the square. The lamps seemed to be dancing away from him now and when he stood in front of the door in the wall it lifted gently then settled into place again. He wrenched it open and lurched along the garden path like a drunken man.

The bell echoed away into the night and he kept on ringing it and then he started to laugh. He knew it was silly but he couldn't stop it, and he leaned against the door, laughing hysterically, so that when it opened he fell inside.

And then he was safe. Her arms were around him and he was safe and warm, and somewhere near at hand he could hear Murphy's voice, high-pitched and excited. But it was Anne Murray's face he saw. Soft and warm and full of love for him. He tried to smile to her and then her face began to recede into the darkness, further and further away, until she had disappeared and he was alone again.

7

He drifted up from a deep pit of darkness into the light. For a little while his vision was blurred and the walls of the room seemed to move in and out. He closed his eyes and then opened them again. There was a quick movement near at hand and Johnny Murphy leaned over him. 'Thank God!' he said fervently and rushed from the room.

Fallon lay staring up at the ceiling. He felt calm and rested, but drained of all strength. After a while he became aware of the dull ache in his side. He moved slightly to ease the strain and closed his eyes again. The door opened with a soft click and there was the rustle of a dress. When he opened his eyes

Anne Murray was leaning over him. He smiled weakly. 'The bad penny again,' he said.

She smiled warmly and sat down on the edge of the bed and took his hand. 'I was never so glad to see anyone in my life,' she said. 'How do you feel?'

He grinned. 'Alive – but only just. How long have I been here?'

'About twelve hours,' she said. 'You passed out when you arrived.'

At that moment the door opened and Murphy came in, carefully balancing a tray. He grinned amiably as the girl put an extra pillow behind Fallon's back, and said, 'Aren't you the great one, Mr Fallon? The whole country's going crazy.'

Fallon frowned and looked at the girl enquiringly. 'It's true,' she told him. 'You've really caused a storm this time.'

'Poor Phil,' Fallon sighed. 'He won't come very well out of this at all.'

Anne Murray nodded. 'Some reporter's already dug up the fact that you were at University together.' She picked up a spoon and said briskly, 'Come on now. Cut out the talking and open your mouth. You need some of this beef stew inside you.' He opened his mouth obediently and she began to spoon stew into his mouth as though he were a child.

Murphy said enthusiastically, 'That was a hell of a thing you did yesterday morning, Mr Fallon. Saving Inspector Stuart like that.' He frowned suddenly, the smile dying on his face. 'That Rogan's a bad one. The sooner they get him the better, I say.'

Fallon swallowed a mouthful of food and held up his hand. 'Do you mean to tell me he's still at large?' he asked incredulously.

Murphy nodded. 'He's pretty smart, I can't deny that.'

Fallon lay back against the pillows, frowning. 'I can't understand how he managed to get out of town.'

'Perhaps he's got another hideout in Castlemore,' Anne Murray said. 'Perhaps he's still here like you are.'

Fallon shook his head. 'No, I don't think so. He hates me. If he'd had anywhere else to go to he'd have gone yesterday morning after planting the bomb in Stuart's car. He came back here for one reason only – he had nowhere else to go.'

'Come on, finish this,' she said, holding out another spoonful, and he opened his mouth obediently.

'That was good,' he said when he had finished.

She smiled and wiped his mouth with a napkin. 'Now drink your milk like a good boy,' she ordered.

He wrinkled his face. 'Not milk – I hate it. To tell you the truth I could just do with a drop of the real stuff.'

'The worst possible thing you could have,' she said and took a glass of warm milk from the tray.

Fallon grimaced. 'All right, but I'll drink it myself, thank you. I'm not finished yet, you know.'

As he sipped the milk Murphy said, 'Well, I'll leave you, Mr Fallon. You could do with some more sleep.'

Fallon made an exclamation of disgust. 'Nothing doing,' he said. 'I'm going to get up when I've finished this. It was only a flesh wound, you know. The doctor told me. I've got to work out our next move.'

Anne smiled and shook her head firmly. 'You aren't going anywhere,' she said. 'You nearly killed yourself last night. How you haven't got pneumonia I don't know.'

He smiled brightly. 'I'd have been in a worse position if I'd stayed.'

Murphy paused on his way to the door and stood quite still. The girl said, 'What do you mean?'

Fallon shrugged. 'I was to be charged as an accessory to murder.' Her breath hissed sharply between her teeth and he turned his head and said to Murphy, 'That means you too, lad. I'm sorry.'

There was a short silence and Murphy said with a forced laugh, 'I suppose it serves us right for not keeping better company, Mr Fallon.' He turned and walked to the door. He hesitated with the door half-open and said slowly, 'Would they – would they hang us if they caught us, Mr Fallon?'

Fallon stared down into his empty glass

and placed it gently on the tray. 'Very probably,' he said.

A tiny moan escaped from the boy's mouth and his shoulders sagged. He remained like that in the doorway for several moments and then he straightened up and said with forced brightness, 'Then we'll have to damn well see they don't get us, won't we, Mr Fallon?'

Fallon nodded and replied in the same tone, 'Don't worry, lad. They won't catch us if I can help it.'

The door closed behind Murphy and Anne said, 'Is it as bad as that? Do you really think they would hang you?'

He wrinkled his brows and smiled slightly. 'I don't know. I'm only going by what Phil Stuart told me. Rogan fixed that booby trap, but we were his accomplices in the eyes of the law – accessories before the fact, they call it. Another thing, if they do catch Rogan, which they very probably will, he'll spill his guts. He'll incriminate me and the boy out of sheer malice.' A sudden thought struck him and he said slowly, 'In fact he'll very probably bring you into it as well.'

There was a short silence while they both thought about what he had just said and then the girl spoke. 'That means we'll have to leave here together,' she said. 'There isn't any other way out, is there? I can't very well stay here to wait for the police, can I?'

He stared at her, dismay on his face, as the full horror of what he had done to her burst upon him. 'I've ruined you,' he said. 'I've ruined you entirely.'

When she replied her voice seemed to come from a great distance. He shook his head violently and she sounded quite normal again. 'Don't worry about me. All I'm worried about is that wound of yours. The blood had seeped through the bandage. It's a good job I was here to render professional service.'

He opened his mouth to reply and then she was very far away and there was a strange buzzing in his ears. 'What's wrong?' he croaked. 'Everything's going round in circles.'

Her voice came from the depths of a whirlpool. 'That's just what should happen. I put something in your milk. Now you can sleep for another twelve hours whether you like it or not.' The darkness swirled over him and she was gone again.

When he awoke the room was dark. He lay there for a moment adjusting his thoughts and then he threw aside the bedclothes and sat on the edge of the bed. The dull ache in his side had abated a little and he was no longer so acutely uncomfortable. He padded across the room and switched on the lights. For a moment his head whirled as an attack of dizziness hit him, but it passed very quickly. There was an old dressing gown lying across the foot of the bed and he slipped it on and left the room.

He quickly passed along the landing and descended the back stairs. He could hear a murmur of voices and he paused a moment before opening the door. Anne Murray and the boy were sitting on either side of the table. There was a chess board between them and Murphy was in the act of moving his queen. Fallon walked over to the table and smiled. 'That's a stupid move,' he said, glancing down at the board. 'You've got to watch yourself when you're dealing with a woman.'

She smiled up at him. 'I'm sorry, but it was the best thing for you – believe me.'

He pulled up a chair and sat down. 'I'm not annoyed,' he said. 'It's just that another day has passed and I haven't made any definite plans. We really are in danger here. They might catch Rogan at any minute and that would be the worst possible thing that could happen from our point of view.'

She smiled and said to Murphy, 'Move the board, will you, Johnny? I'll make some supper.' Murphy began to put the pieces into a box and she walked over to the stove and said, 'You aren't the only one who's capable of thinking, you know. What would you say if I told you it was all worked out?'

He looked up in surprise. 'What do you mean?'

She opened the cupboard and started to take things out. 'You tell him, Johnny,' she said. 'These master-minds hate to have to listen to a woman.'

Murphy grinned and took out a map. 'It's

a pretty good idea, Mr Fallon,' he said, 'and Anne – Miss Murray, I mean – has worked it out herself. With a little assistance from me, that is.'

Fallon raised his eyebrows. 'You two must have got very friendly,' he observed coldly.

Murphy blushed and hastily unfolded the map. 'This idea is based on something that's happening here tomorrow. Miss Murray sold some of the furniture to a dealer from Stramore last week. It's all piled up in the front room waiting. He's coming tomorrow morning with a removal van.'

Fallon's interest was aroused immediately. 'Go on,' he said, leaning forward.

Murphy grinned. 'That's really the most important part of the plan, Mr Fallon. It's our way out of town. The place is crawling with peelers. They'll be having a house-to-house search next. Stuart must be convinced you're still in town. When the furniture men have loaded the van tomorrow, or at some other convenient time, Miss Murray will call them into the kitchen for tea. Them fellas never refuse. You know what they're like.

You and I can hide ourselves amongst the stuff in the back.'

There was a short silence as the boy looked eagerly into Fallon's face. Fallon nodded gravely. 'All right. Let's suppose it works and we pass through the road blocks. What then?'

The boy nodded. 'That's where Miss Murray comes in. She'll get through the road blocks with no trouble at all. She's hired a car. It's out in the garage now, and tomorrow she'll follow the van. At the first opportunity we'll hop out and she'll pick us up. We can try to cross over into Donegall then,' he added.

There was a long silence and Fallon leaned over and studied the map. After a while he said, 'Yes, it's quite a good plan. Not bad at all – so far as it goes.'

Anne Murray pushed a cup in front of him, slopping tea into the saucer, and said indignantly, 'All right, master-mind. What's wrong with it?'

He raised a hand in a gesture of defence. 'Don't get me wrong,' he said. 'It is a good plan, but it needs tightening up a little, that's all.'

He sipped a little of his tea and leaned back. 'For instance – what happens if you develop engine trouble? We can't very well ask our driver to stop and we don't want to use intimidation because that gives Stuart a direct lead to our whereabouts.'

She snorted. 'All right. I suppose it could happen, but it isn't very likely.'

He nodded his head. 'I agree, but believe me, it's the unexpected that always happens. You've got to make allowances for every possible contingency. It's only forty miles to Stramore. What if the driver doesn't stop? And remember, Murphy and I can't just drop over the tailboard at any busy road junction where the van happens to slow – it would look too suspicious.'

A dejected look appeared on the boy's face and Anne Murphy said slowly, 'Yes, I suppose you've got something there.'

Fallon smiled and slapped Murphy on the shoulder. 'Don't lose heart,' he said. 'I told you it only needed a few extras.' He leaned over the map and studied it for a while and then he said, 'Right, this is what we'll do. We'll follow your plan as far as it will work. If anything happens to stop Murphy and me from leaving the van between here and Stramore we'll have to sit tight and take our chances.' He turned to the boy. 'Do you have a safe address in Stramore? Somewhere that would take us off the streets during daylight or where we could spend the night if necessary?'

Murphy frowned and then his face brightened. 'Sure there's Conroy's, Mr Fallon,' he said. 'I've taken messages there many a time.'

Fallon laughed in amazement. 'Is that old devil still in business?' He shook his head and considered. 'I never could trust him. It's anything for a fiver with him, and I'm worth two thousand.'

'Five thousand.' Murphy coughed and said apologetically, 'That's the reward they've announced for the arrest of the man responsible for the booby trap killing.'

'The rate's gone up, has it?' Fallon said. For a brief moment he stared into space and he smiled crookedly. 'Ah, well, Conroy's it must be.'

'But what will I do if I miss you and you do have to go to this man Conroy?' Anne demanded.

'I'm coming to that,' he told her. 'You must book in at a hotel in Stramore for the night. Tell them you'll be making an early start the next day and pay in advance.' He looked down at the map again and continued. 'Just outside Stramore on the main road to the north there's a ruined castle with a wood beyond it. A side road cuts through that wood and about a quarter of a mile along it, there's an old, humpbed-back bridge. We'll meet you there.'

'At what time?' she said.

He shrugged his shoulders. 'Oh, about eleven o'clock. The cinemas come out about ten-thirty. There'll be quite a few people about. That will give us good cover for getting out of town.'

'But why can't I pick you up in Stramore when I leave my hotel?' she said.

He shook his head and said gently, 'It's getting to be just a little too hot. By now they'll have Murphy's description as well. It just needs one observant passer-by – just one.'

There was finality in his voice when he went on, 'No, we'll meet you outside the town as I've just described.'

She opened her mouth to protest and Murphy said, 'I agree with him, Miss Murray.'

For a moment she glared at them and then she shrugged her shoulders in resignation. 'All right. Have it your own way.'

She made a meal of eggs and fried ham and Fallon wolfed it down as if he hadn't eaten for days. Afterwards they sat talking over coffee and after a while Murphy said, 'Well, I think I'll hit the hay. I want to be at my best for tomorrow.' He smiled and left the kitchen.

'He's a nice kid,' Fallon said.

Anne nodded. 'It hasn't got him very far, has it?'

Fallon sighed. 'I know, but it isn't entirely my fault. He was mixed up in the Organization before I ever arrived on the scene.' He lit a cigarette and blew smoke out thoughtfully. 'He's got a fine mind. Doesn't like the violence at all and he's loyal. Nearly sacrificed himself to save me the other night.' He sighed. 'I hope to God I can get him safe across the border.'

'I hope you get Martin Fallon safely across the border,' she said.

'And you?' he said, 'What about you?'

She shrugged and said quietly, 'If I'm lucky and Rogan doesn't talk when they catch him I'll be able to carry on with my plans, I suppose. Go back to London. If it doesn't work out that way . . .'

Her voice trailed off and Fallon said harshly, 'It will if I can get to Rogan before the police do.'

'And what would you do?' she said.

'Kill him. It's all that he deserves.'

She shook her head sadly. 'And you came across the border to save him. What a stupid business it all is.' He nodded without replying and she said with a determined gaiety, 'But what if I do have to cross the border? Where will I go? What will I do?'

He considered the point for a moment and said slowly, 'You could come to Cavan to my cottage.'

'Would I like it there?' she said.

He laughed. 'You'd like it very much. It's only half a mile over the border. You can see it from the border post at Doone. It's a grand place. The air's like wine and the sky over the mountain changes its face every five minutes just to entertain you.'

'Why did you ever leave it if you were so happy there?' she said, shaking her head.

He grinned in puzzlement. 'I wish to God I knew. I was a bit lonely, I'll grant you that, and I was drinking more than was good for me, but there was something else. Some malaise of the spirit.' He screwed up his eyes and stared back into the past and then he stood up and said abruptly, 'Murphy has the right idea. We ought to go to bed.'

She nodded, a curious expression on her face, but made no reply. He put out the light and they went upstairs together. When they reached her door they paused and she smiled and said, 'Well – good night.' A sudden tightness clutched at his throat. He opened his mouth to reply and then she slipped a hand behind his neck and pulled down his head. Her lips touched his mouth, slightly parted, draining the strength out of him, and as he reached out for her, the door banged and she had gone. He stood looking at her door for a long time before he turned, with his mind in a turmoil, and walked slowly along to his own room.

He slept very soundly, a fact which surprised him considering the amount of sleep he'd had during the previous two days, but he decided that his wound must have sapped his strength more than he had realized. He was awakened by Murphy with a cup of tea at seven-thirty. The boy smiled and said, 'It's another hell of a day, Mr Fallon. I don't think it's ever going to stop raining.'

Fallon swallowed the tea gratefully. He handed the cup back to Murphy and started to get out of bed and a sudden thought struck him and he groaned. 'My God!' he said. 'I haven't any clothes. I forgot clean about it.'

Murphy grinned and shook his head. 'It's all right. She thought of that. Yesterday afternoon when you were sleeping she went shopping. If you'll look in the cupboard you'll find a pair of trousers and a shirt. You left the jacket of your suit when you ran out so unexpectedly.'

He left the room and Fallon went into the bathroom and washed and shaved. His side was still very sore and stiff and his arm felt curiously numb. He swung it a few times to restore the circulation and then he dressed. When he put his jacket on, the Luger was back in its usual place. He took it out and hefted it in his hand. There was a comforting feel to it. He wondered what would have happened if he'd taken it with him that morning when he had gone to warn Stuart. He smiled grimly. One thing was certain – he would have been dead now. He slipped the weapon back into the holster and went downstairs.

Breakfast was ready and waiting. He sniffed at the aroma of frying bacon and said, 'That smells good.'

She turned to greet him, her eyes crinkling. 'How do you feel this morning?'

He grinned. 'Not so bad. A bit stiff, but it looks as if I'll survive.'

She put plates before them and they began to eat. When they were finished Fallon said, 'What time will they be here?'

'Ten o'clock,' she told him and began to clear the table. When she had finished she went out into the hall and came back wearing her raincoat. 'I'm going out for an hour,' she said.

Fallon looked up in surprise. 'Is it important?'

She nodded. 'I'm going round to see Philip Stuart's wife, Jane. If he calls and finds I've gone without leaving a message he'll think it's peculiar. Might even start trying to trace me.'

Fallon nodded. 'Yes, you're right. Careful you don't stay too long. It would ruin everything if you were late, and bring a newspaper back with you,' he called as she went out of the front door.

It was half-past nine when she returned. Fallon and Murphy were deeply engrossed in a game of chess. She entered the kitchen and took them by surprise. 'A fine pair you are,' she said. 'What if I'd been the police?'

'To a peeler as pretty as you we'd have surrendered without a murmur,' Murphy said impudently.

She smiled beautifully, her whole face lighting up, and handed Fallon a newspaper. He opened it at once. He wasn't a headline, but there was a large piece in the right-hand corner of the front page. It simply said that police were still searching and had every reason to believe he was still in Castlemore. Extra men had been drafted in from other parts of the province. There was a small paragraph about Rogan, who had apparently disappeared off the face of the earth, and a line on Murphy who, it was stated, was believed to be with either Fallon or Rogan.

Fallon looked up and smiled slightly. 'Not so good,' he said. 'They've brought extra police in.'

She nodded. 'I know. Jane Stuart told me.' Anne sighed and took off her coat. 'I felt a bit low sitting there, letting her give me confidences when all the time I knew exactly where you were.'

'Has my escape affected Phil's position much?' Fallon said.

She shook her head. 'Apparently not. One or two stupid remarks in some of the English papers. Muck-raking, as usual. No, his integrity is too well known for anyone to think there was any collusion between you. Most of the Irish papers seem to think it's rather amusing that you were friends in your young days.'

Fallon sighed with relief. 'I'm glad I haven't harmed him,' he said.

She shook her head. 'From what Jane said to me he's rather more than half pleased that you got away. He was absolutely dumb-founded when they told him you'd escaped. He said when he left, you looked incapable of crossing the room.'

Before he could reply the bell rang shrilly. Anne hurried along the hall to the door. She peered out through the wide window and then rushed back. 'It's the furniture men,' she said. 'You'd better get upstairs. I'll let you know when they're almost through.'

They hurriedly mounted the back stairs and took refuge in Fallon's bedroom. Fallon took out his cigarettes and they lit up and sat on the bed waiting. For a little while Fallon watched from behind the curtain as the men struggled down the garden path with various items of furniture. There were two of them and they appeared to be taking their time.

Three-quarters of an hour passed and Fallon began to stir impatiently and then the door opened and the girl appeared. 'They're taking the last piece out now,' she said. 'I've got the tea ready in the kitchen and I've already asked them in. They were only too pleased.'

He nodded. 'Don't forget to scream for help if you need it,' he said facetiously.

She laughed lightly. 'They're both old enough to be my father.'

He gently took her hands. 'Look after yourself,' he said.

The smile died on her face and she replied soberly, 'I pray to God everything goes off all right.'

'It will do,' Murphy said brightly. 'Have no fear of that.'

191

She smiled at him and then looked again at Fallon. For a moment her eyes spoke to him and then she whispered, 'Good luck!' and left the room.

They waited on the landing until the voices of the two men had faded into the kitchen and Fallon pulled on his trench coat and rain hat and they went quickly downstairs. The boy was wearing his old leather motoring coat and Fallon said, 'That's a hell of a conspicuous thing to wear, you know.'

Murphy shrugged. 'I suppose you're right, Mr Fallon. If it would only stop raining I'd throw it away.' He laughed gaily at his own joke and Fallon smiled. They went out into the road and stood at the rear of the van.

Fallon looked around casually. 'Nobody about. That's good.' The men had already hooked the tailboard into place and he said, 'Right! Now take it down and we'll climb up nice and easy, just in case anybody happens to be looking out of a window.'

Murphy nodded. They lowered the tailboard and pulled it up after them when they had clambered into the van. Anne Murray's furniture only half-filled it and had been positioned well to the back. Sacking was plentifully draped over everything. Murphy went burrowing in amongst the stacked furniture and gave an exclamation of triumph. 'In here, Mr Fallon,' he said. 'We couldn't be safer.'

Fallon ducked between the legs of a table and Murphy held up a flap of sacking, disclosing a small corner a few feet square, between a wardrobe and the side of the van. Murphy pulled a few more sacks in and Fallon nodded with satisfaction. 'That's fine. When we approach the road blocks we'll cover ourselves with those.'

They sat down on the sacks and waited and about ten minutes later they heard the voices of the two men as they approached the van. They climbed up into the cab and a moment later the engine roared into life. Fallon crept out of the hiding place and peered over the edge of the tailboard. As they bumped across the square a green Hillman saloon turned out of the drive at the side of the house and moved after them. He smiled with satisfaction and crawled back underneath the table. 'She's on our tail,' he said. 'From now on all we can do is keep our fingers crossed.'

For five or six minutes the van moved at a steady rate through the traffic and then it started to slow. For a little while it was only crawling along and Fallon and the boy lay curled up in the small space and pulled the sacks over them.

Fallon had his ear to the side of the van. He heard a voice ask the driver where he was coming from. There was an indistinct reply and then there was the sound of steps going round to the back of the van. There was a scraping sound as someone heaved himself up and looked over the tailboard, and then he dropped back into the road with a clatter. The steps moved back to the cab and a second later the engine started up again, and the van moved off. For several minutes Fallon and the boy lay there under the sacks and then Murphy pulled them away and said in a low voice, 'We've done it, Mr Fallon. We've fooled the bloody peelers.'

Fallon grinned and held up a warning

hand. 'Yes, we've done it, but keep your voice down for God's sake.'

They crawled out from underneath the table and Fallon lit a cigarette with a sigh of relief. He felt marvellous. It really looked as if they might get away with it. He crawled to the rear of the van and peered over the edge of the tailboard. They were rattling along through the rain at a steady speed between thorn hedges. The countryside stretched green and lush through the light mist on either side of them. It looked beautiful. There was only one thing missing, Anne Murray in her green Hillman saloon.

8

Murphy crouched glumly by the tailboard looking back along the road. There wasn't very much traffic. Occasionally a fast car overtook them, but there was no sign of the green Hillman. He glanced at his watch. They had been on the way for more than an hour. He turned to Fallon who sat on a sack, his back against a sideboard, and said, 'There isn't a sign of her, Mr Fallon. What are we going to do?'

Fallon shrugged. 'What can we do?' He laughed at the crestfallen expression on the boy's face and said, 'I warned you this might happen. It could be anything. She might have taken a wrong turning, or punctured a tyre, or even run out of petrol, though I admit that isn't very probable.' He grinned and punched the boy in the shoulder. 'Don't worry. We'll see what happens in Stramore. We'll drop off this thing at the first opportunity and go to Conroy's place. We'll pick Anne up tonight, never fear.'

Murphy seemed reassured and subsided on to the floor. Fallon moved across to the tailboard and lit a cigarette. As he smoked he looked back along the road. He was more anxious than he wanted Murphy to know. He was worried about Anne Murray personally and about what might have happened to delay her. His thoughts dwelt for a moment on road accidents and crashes and he pushed them hastily away and sighed deeply. It was no use worrying. They could only wait and see.

They were still waiting when the van entered Stramore. The town was busy, for it was market day, and the van had to slow down to a crawl as it moved through the heavy traffic and the crowds. It turned into a side street and halted. Fallon and Murphy hastily crawled back into their hiding place. As they listened they heard the two men climb down from the cab and walk away, their voices dying into the distance. There was a moment of silence and Fallon said, 'Let's get out of here.' They crawled out from under the table and hastily clambered over the tail-board and dropped down into the street.

The van was standing outside some terrace houses and there was a small public house several doors away. Murphy grinned. 'You wouldn't have to look far for them two,' he said.

They hesitated for a moment on the corner of the street and Fallon said, 'You'd better lead the way. It's a long time since I was lost in this town.' Murphy nodded and stepped off the pavement into the road and they were immediately swept up by the swirling mass of people who filled the streets.

They couldn't have picked a better day. The town was thronged with country folk, in for the day. There were cattle pens and market stalls set up in the gutters lining the pavements and the air was raucous with the cries of the vendors. They moved with the crowd, keeping a careful watch for the police, and on two occasions changed course abruptly to avoid a constable on duty.

They crossed the market place and turned into a side street. There were fewer people about and they began to walk rapidly. Murphy led the way long a back street that finally opened into a small square. One side of the square was taken up by a large shabby-looking brick house over a shop with a yard at the side of it. An ancient notice, faded and weatherbeaten, jutted out from the wall bearing the legend: Paddy Conroy – General Dealer.

Fallon looked up at the sign and grinned. 'That's the right description for him,' he said. 'The old bastard's as crooked as a donkey's hind leg. He'll handle anything that will bring him a shilling.'

Murphy looked worried. 'Will we be all right here, do you think, Mr Fallon?'

Fallon frowned. 'We've no choice at the moment.' He laughed grimly. 'I know one thing – if he makes a wrong move I'll put a bullet through him. He's earned one years ago.'

He pushed open the shop door and Murphy followed him in. An ancient bell jangled brassily somewhere in the rear of the house and still sounded after Murphy had closed the door. The shop was piled with a mass of other people's unwanted rubbish and an unpleasant smell lingered over everything. Murphy shook his head. 'Do you think he makes a living out of this stuff, Mr Fallon?' he said.

Fallon shrugged. 'Your guess is as good as mine.'

The sound of the bell finally died away and there was a silence. Flies buzzed in the grimy window and Fallon pushed his hat back from his forehead and wiped sweat from his brow. There was a movement at the rear of the shop and a door opened. A young girl stood watching them. She looked about eighteen or twenty and was pretty in a bold, sluttish way. She had a weak, full mouth and a ripe figure. 'What is it?' she demanded ungraciously.

Fallon smiled pleasantly. 'Is Mr Conroy at home, my dear?'

'He's at the pub,' she said, 'but he'll be in for his dinner at any moment. Is it something you wanted to buy?'

Fallon shook his head. 'I'm an old friend just passing through town. I thought I'd look him up. I haven't seen him in years.'

There was a puzzled frown on her face and her eyes flickered to Murphy. For a moment she stared at him and her expression changed. 'I've seen you before,' she said.

Murphy nodded. 'That's right, me darlin',' he said impudently. 'I was here last month with a message for your dad.'

Her eyes widened. 'You've come from the Organization.' For a moment longer she looked at Murphy and then she turned again to Fallon and a sudden recognition came into her eyes. She stepped forward and her face glowed. 'You're Martin Fallon,' she breathed. 'I've seen your picture in the papers. You're the one the peelers are running round in circles looking for.'

He nodded and produced his most charming

smile. 'That's right, my dear. I've come to see if your dad will put me up for the night. Do you think he will?'

He moved round behind the counter and smiled down at her and she nodded vigorously. 'We'll be proud to give you shelter, Mr Fallon.'

Fallon nodded and moved very close until their bodies were almost touching. 'You'll be Rose,' he said. 'The last time I was here you were only a little girl. Now you're a young woman.' She gazed up at him, a look of adoration on her face, and he went on, 'Can I trust you, Rose?'

'Oh, yes, Mr Fallon,' she breathed.

A peculiar, intimate little smile appeared on his face and he leaned closer and said, 'I'm in great danger, Rose. If the wrong word was spoken – a careless word, even – I'd be taken. You wouldn't want that to happen, would you?'

For a moment her eyes closed. She shivered in a sort of ecstasy and her young breasts quivered. 'They'll not hear it from me, Mr Fallon. Not if they used red hot pincers.'

For a moment he smiled down into her face and then he patted her arm. 'I knew I could rely on you,' he told her.

'You'd best come into the back room,' she said. 'Someone might come in the shop.'

She led the way along a dark corridor, her hips moving rhythmically, tainting the air with a faint animal odour as she passed. Fallon sighed. He hadn't enjoyed his performance but the girl's reaction had been so obvious. He couldn't afford to lose such an important ally.

She led the way into a shabby living-room and said, 'Make yourselves comfortable. I'll put a few more spuds in the pot for dinner.'

She disappeared into the kitchen, closing the door behind her, and Murphy threw down his coat and whistled. 'She looks no better than she ought to be,' he said. 'But what were you doing, Mr Fallon, playing up to her?'

Fallon shrugged. 'She probably goes to the cinema too much and thinks gunmen are romantic. I couldn't afford to turn all that devotion down.' He threw himself into a chair and added, 'Don't forget her old man is a slippery customer. Rose might come in very useful to us yet.'

Murphy shook his head and grinned. 'Watch yourself, Mr Fallon. She fell for you in a big way. You might have a job getting rid of her.'

The door behind them opened with a bang and Fallon jumped to his feet, the Luger appearing in his hand as if by magic. Paddy Conroy stood facing them, mouth wide open in his blotched, whisky face. 'Holy Mother of God!' he said in a whisper.

Fallon pushed the Luger back into its holster and smiled genially. 'Is it yourself, Paddy?' He walked across the room and held out his hand. 'It's been a long time.'

Conroy took the hand mechanically. 'It has indeed, Mr Fallon,' he said in a faraway voice. He blinked his rheumy eyes several times and Fallon's nose wrinkled in disgust at the stale, beery smell that surrounded him. Suddenly Conroy came to life and a look of horror came into his eyes. 'Jesus help us!' he cried. 'I'd better close the shop in case someone comes in.' He rushed along the passage and disappeared from sight.

Murphy raised his eyebrows. 'That'll be the day, when he gets a customer in here,' he said.

Fallon grinned and Rose came in from the kitchen and laid the table. She had smeared a vivid orange lipstick on her mouth and she wore a pair of cheap, patent-leather, high-heeled shoes. She smiled provocatively and swayed back into the kitchen. Fallon stared helplessly at Murphy who collapsed on the couch exploding with laughter as Conroy came back into the room. 'It's an honour to have you here, Mr Fallon. An honour, sir. The great things you've done for Ireland in the last few days.' A drop quivered on the end of his nose as he added piously, 'You'll go down in history, Mr Fallon. In history.'

Fallon managed a smile. 'And where's your wife, Paddy?' he said. 'I forgot to ask after her when we arrived.'

An expression of pain and sorrow appeared on Conroy's face. 'Gone!' he said. 'She's left me, Mr Fallon, after all these years together.'

'Has she run out on you, then?' Murphy said with interest.

Conroy looked pained. 'I mean she's passed on to a happier land, young man,' he said reprovingly. He sighed deeply and produced a bottle from behind a cushion. 'But these things are sent to try us, I suppose. Would you like a drop of the hard stuff, Mr Fallon?' Fallon shook his head and the man raised the bottle to his mouth and swallowed deeply.

The door opened and Rose came in from the kitchen carrying a tray loaded with plates of food. 'Will you sit down, Mr Fallon?' she said, putting a generously heaped plate down at the head of the table.

Her father rubbed his hands together and said, 'Yes, indeed, Mr Fallon. Sit you down. It's only humble fare but I'm a poor man. A poor man.'

Surprisingly the food was quite good and Fallon and Murphy tucked into it without further conversation. The meal passed in silence punctuated by the various unpleasant slobbering sounds without which Conroy seemed unable to pass food into his mouth. When they had finished Fallon pushed back his plate and said, 'That was a fine meal, Rose. As good as I've ever tasted.'

She coloured and started to clear the plates and her father leered and said, 'Aye, she'll make some lucky lad a fine wife.' He grinned evilly and rammed his elbow into Fallon's side. 'Believe me, Mr Fallon, cooking isn't her only virtue.'

Fallon stifled his disgust and managed a smile as the girl brought in the tea. She looked near to tears and he guessed that she'd heard her father's remark. Murphy got up and said, 'Come on, Rose. I'll give you a hand with the dishes,' and he grinned at Fallon and followed her into the kitchen.

Conroy belched and began to pick his teeth with a matchstalk. He leaned back in his chair. 'Well, now, Mr Fallon. It's a hornets' nest you've stirred up this time, and no mistake.'

Fallon took out a cigarette and said calmly, 'I've stirred them up before.'

The old man nodded. 'I'm not denying it, but never to such an extent as this.'

Fallon leaned forward, his eyes narrowing.

'All right, Paddy. Let's have it. What have you heard?'

Conroy took out an old clay pipe and began to fill it from a rubber pouch. 'They've got the troops out this time, Mr Fallon.' He paused to light his pipe and when it was drawing properly, went on. 'If you're thinking of trying for Donegall, forget it. They've not only got the soldiers between here and the border; the polis are out in these armoured cars they've got now. Terrible things they are, with fancy radios. You wouldn't stand a chance.'

Fallon nodded slowly, his face impassive. Inside his thoughts were racing. It was a mess. Much worse than he had imagined. He smiled and said, 'Not to worry, Paddy. I've got plans.' He leaned across and patted Conroy on the knee and added, 'With friends he can trust a man can go a long way.'

Conroy nodded vigorously. 'Indeed he can, Mr Fallon.' He paused and examined the stem of his pipe. 'There's the reward of course.' He looked up hastily and added, 'Not that I'm suggesting anyone would betray you,

Mr Fallon, but five thousand pounds is a terrible amount of money.'

Fallon nodded calmly. 'That's true enough,' he said. 'Of course it's not much use if you can't spend it. I don't think the Organization would let the man who earned it live long enough to enjoy it.'

There was a short, pregnant silence and Conroy sighed. 'Aye, you're right there, Mr Fallon.' For a moment longer he stared deeply into space and then he pulled himself together and said brightly, 'But let's discuss the important things, Mr Fallon. How long will you be staying with us?'

A small warning voice spoke inside Fallon and he said warily, 'I'm not sure. Certainly until tomorrow night.' In his wallet he still had more than a hundred pounds left of the money O'Hara had given him. He took it out now and extracted ten pounds, displaying the rest ostentatiously. Conroy's eyes gleamed and Fallon pushed the money across. 'That's a little something on account, Paddy. Naturally, I'll have a little more for you later on.'

'There was no need, Mr Fallon. No need

at all,' Conroy said. His hands reached across the table and fastened over the two five pound notes.

The kitchen door opened and Murphy entered. 'Well, that's my good deed done for the day,' he said. 'What happens now?'

Conroy heaved himself to his feet. 'I think you'd better go upstairs, Mr Fallon,' he said. 'One of the neighbours might come in. It wouldn't do to stay here.'

For a moment Fallon looked directly into his eyes and Conroy smiled nervously. 'All right, Paddy,' Fallon said. 'Anything you say.'

Conroy nodded. 'It'll be the safest thing. Rose will show you the way.' He sank down on the couch again and Rose led the way out of the room.

They followed her up a creaking, un-carpeted stairway that led to a narrow landing. There were only four doors leading off it. Fallon paused at the bottom of the next flight of stairs and said, 'What about the attics?'

The girl shook her head. 'The stairs are rotten up there, Mr Fallon.' She gestured scornfully downstairs and said, 'He keeps meaning to get them fixed but he never gets around to it.' She opened the first door and they were met by a frightful stench. She wrinkled her nose and closed the door gently. 'That's his room. I don't suppose you want to go in there.'

'No thanks,' Murphy said. 'I don't think we'd survive.'

She opened the next door and they walked into a tiny room, half-filled with junk. There was a truckle bed in one corner with a mattress on it. 'Is this the best you can do?' Murphy said.

'You can sleep there,' she said calmly. 'Mr Fallon can use my room.' Murphy opened his mouth to make an indignant reply but Fallon frowned quickly and they followed the girl out of the room. She gestured to a door opposite and said, 'That's the bathroom,' and then she flung open the end door and announced with pride in her voice, 'This is my room.'

There was a threadbare carpet on the floor and a narrow bed over by the window covered with a cheap satin quilt. Against one wall an ancient Victorian dressing table stood. The girl had made some attempt to camouflage it with a bilious looking chintz material and the experiment was a notable failure. The rest of the walls were covered with pin-up pictures of her cinema idols. Fallon moved into the room and said, 'It's very nice indeed.'

She smiled her delight. 'Oh, I knew you'd like it, Mr Fallon.' She moved towards the door. 'I'll have to go now. I've some shopping to do in the market.'

Fallon followed her out into the corridor making a sign to Murphy to stay in the room. He walked with her to the head of the stairs and they paused. 'Can I trust you, Rose?' he said.

Her face glowed and she nodded vigorously. 'I'll not let you down, Mr Fallon.'

He squeezed her arm. 'You'll let me know if you see anything suspicious going on?' She nodded again and he said, 'Good girl!'

She started to descend the stairs. Half-way down she turned and smiled up at him. 'I'll watch me Dad for you, too, Mr Fallon,' she said.

He stood listening to the click of her absurd high heels until they faded away into the living room and then he returned to Murphy. The boy was working his way along the walls looking at the pin-ups. 'She's got a hell of a taste, Mr Fallon,' he said.

'Thank you!' Fallon said dryly.

Murphy turned with a grin. 'Now then, Mr Fallon, you know what I mean.' His face became serious and he sat down on the bed. 'What do you think about Conroy?'

Fallon sat down beside him. 'He's about as trustworthy as a snake,' he said. 'But I think he's more frightened of what the Organization might do to him if he betrays us than anything else.'

Murphy shook his head. 'I don't know. Five thousand pounds is a lot of money. A hell of a lot of money.' For a moment he was silent and then he said, 'What's our next move?'

Fallon leaned back against the wall. 'We'll hang on here as arranged until tonight, then we'll go and meet Anne.'

'And after that?' Murphy said.

214

'I'm not sure.' Fallon frowned. 'Things are pretty sticky up here. I thought it would be easier to cross the border into Donegall but Conroy says they've got the soldiers out. Another thing, the police are patrolling the border in armoured cars with short wave radio sets. It makes it damned difficult.'

'We're in a hell of a fix then,' Murphy said.

Fallon nodded. 'We'd be better going south again. It might be easier to cross where there's plenty of coming and going.' He frowned as he considered the problem. 'We really need somewhere to hide up for a day or two until the search has fanned out a bit.' A thought came to him and he sat bolt upright. 'Did you ever hear anyone speak of Hannah Costello?'

Murphy frowned. 'No, I can't say I've ever heard the name mentioned.'

Fallon jumped up and walked to the window. 'She might be dead now,' he said. 'I haven't been near her in ten or twelve years.' He turned and explained. 'She had a farm with a few acres of land in the Sperrin

Mountains. A funny sort of place. It's in a lonely little valley that you would never think existed.' He laughed reminiscently. 'I remember the first time I stayed there. It was about fourteen or fifteen years ago. We'd pulled a job in Derry and the country was raised against us. She put me up for three weeks – charged handsomely, mind you. She was in it for money – not patriotism.'

'And you think she might still be alive?' Murphy said.

Fallon shrugged. 'Who knows? She had two sons, mind you.' He nodded his head and said firmly, 'I think it would be worth a try.' He walked over to the bed and yawned hugely. 'I feel damned tired,' he said. 'I can't understand it.'

Murphy nodded sympathetically. 'It'll be that wound, Mr Fallon. You can't take a knock like that and expect to be over it in a couple of days.' He stood up and said, 'You take a nap for a while and I'll keep watch. Don't worry. I'll wake you at the first sign of anything funny.'

He left the room, closing the door softly

behind him and Fallon lay back on the bed and closed his eyes. The pillow smelt of the cheap scent that Rose imagined was alluring. He thought about the girl and sighed. What a lousy life she must have had. A drunken old villain for a father and a fleapit for a home. Her only outlet was her dreams of romance and adventure, her visits to the cinema, and her cheap magazines. Now he had crossed her path, a gunman on the run. Front-page news. He sighed and stretched to ease the tight feeling round his chest. All she would ever get out of life would be a husband something like her father. A drunken idle rogue who would kick her from pillar to post. He smiled wryly and decided that sometimes life stank to high heaven. He switched his thoughts to Anne Murray and drifted pleasantly into sleep thinking about her.

When he awoke it was dark. The cheap luminous dial of the clock beside the bed showed half-past six. He swung his legs to the floor and stood up. He left the room and quietly went next door. When he turned on the light Murphy was sleeping peacefully, a magazine across his chest. For a moment Fallon debated whether to wake him and then he closed the door and returned to the girl's room. He had hardly closed the door when it opened and she entered carrying a cup of tea. 'I came in before but you were asleep,' she said.

Fallon sat down on the bed and sipped the hot tea gratefully. She stood watching him eagerly. She was wearing an old velvet housecoat that trailed on the floor. He decided that her father had probably picked it up at a sale with a load of other stuff. After a while he said, 'Where's your dad?'

Her expression changed. 'He's been drinking all afternoon,' she said. 'He's in the kitchen, stinking drunk.'

She sat down on the bed beside Fallon and the housecoat fell away exposing her legs. She crossed one deliberately over the other, showing a band of flesh at the top of her stockings and said, 'He makes me sick.'

Fallon put his cup down carefully, his eyes avoiding the legs. 'Yes, he's not a pretty sight at the best of times.' He started to get up.

She grabbed hold of his arm and held him down. 'But I am, aren't I, Mr Fallon?' Before he could reply she threw her arms round his neck and cried, 'Take me with you when you go. I can't stand this hole any more.'

For a moment he struggled with her and finally managed to disengage himself from her grasp. 'It wouldn't be possible,' he said.

She jumped up and untying the sash at her waist, pulled open the housecoat. Underneath she was wearing only the stockings. 'Take me with you,' she begged. 'I'll do anything for you. Anything!'

He gazed at her, a terrible pity welling up inside him, and then he stood up and pulled the housecoat together again, covering her young body. 'I'm sorry,' he said gently. 'But it's still impossible.'

For a moment she stared at him in disbelief and then sudden fury appeared on her face. She slapped him hard and turned and stumbled from the room, sobbing. For several seconds he stood looking at the door and then he sat down on the bed, filled with loathing and self-disgust. He had been to blame. From the start he had acted as if she had been the only girl in the world for him. He cursed savagely and the door clicked open again. When he looked up she was standing framed in the doorway. Her voice was broken by sobs but she was obviously trying hard to control them. 'I wasn't going to tell you unless you'd take me away with you,' she said. 'But I can't keep silent.' She gulped and struggled for words and Fallon stood up quickly. 'It's me Dad,' she explained. 'He intends to go to the polis. He's going to get you to leave the house by a trick and they'll be waiting at the end of the street. That way he thinks the Organization won't ever find out.'

Fallon walked towards her. 'Thank you,' he said, but she turned and fled before he could say anything more.

He went into the next room and shook Murphy. The boy came awake instantly, an expression of alarm on his face. He sat up blinking for a moment and then said with a crestfallen expression. 'My God, did I fall asleep?'

'Never mind,' Fallon said. 'Conroy's going to inform on us. We'll have to fix him quickly before he decides to leave the house.'

They quietly descended the stairs and went into the living-room. It was empty. Alarm moved inside Fallon and he quickly opened the kitchen door. He sighed with relief. Conroy was sprawled in an old armchair, a bottle in one hand. There was a clothes-line hanging from a nail by the door and Fallon took it down and walked across to the chair. Conroy turned at the noise. He was completely drunk but when he saw the clothes-line in Fallon's hand, an expression of alarm flickered in his eyes. He tried to get up and opened his mouth to cry out and Fallon hit him hard on the point of the chin. The old man subsided into his chair.

It was the work of a moment or two to tie him up and they carried him upstairs between them and deposited him on his bed. When Fallon went back to the girl's room the door was locked. He hesitated for a moment outside and then he followed Murphy downstairs.

The rest of the evening passed without incident. Murphy sat by the fire reading magazines and Fallon sprawled in a chair, smoking and thinking. They had a few sandwiches for supper, which Murphy made, and at ten o'clock they began to get ready to move.

Fallon went upstairs and knocked on the door of the girl's bedroom. After a while she opened it. 'What do you want?' she said in a dull voice.

He opened his wallet and took out twenty pounds. 'I want you to take this,' he said. She started to protest but he took her hand and pressed the money into it. 'Promise me you'll leave here at the first opportunity. That's not much, I know, but it will keep you for three or four weeks in Belfast till you get a job.'

For a little while she looked at the money in an uncomprehending way and then she raised her eyes and they were shining. 'I will, Mr Fallon. Oh, I will!'

He squeezed her hand. 'Good girl. We're leaving now. You'll find your father tied up on his bed. Free him in an hour or two.

We don't want him dying on us.' She nodded slowly and then tears started to her eyes and she turned back into her room and closed the door.

It was just on half-past ten when they left the house and threaded their way through the streets. It had stopped raining for a while but the sky was dark with no stars. As they came into the main street the crowds were emerging from the cinemas and Fallon and the boy hurried with them along the streets towards the edge of the town.

They walked rapidly without talking and in about twenty minutes were on the outskirts of Stramore. Now and then a car flashed by in the darkness and they merged into the ditch until it was past. Fallon gave an exclamation of satisfaction as the dark mass of the ruined castle loomed out of the darkness on their right. A few minutes later they had turned into the side road and were hurrying along through the dark wood.

They could hear the water of the stream as it rushed over the stones before they could see the bridge. There was no other sound and

Fallon felt afraid. He began to run forward into the darkness. The bridge loomed out of the night and he paused and said softly, 'Anne! Are you there?'

There was the rattle of a loose stone and then Anne Murray spoke from the darkness. 'Thank God you're here. I've been worried sick.'

Fallon walked forward and his outstretched hands met hers and clung to them for an unspoken moment and Murphy said cheerfully, 'What happened to you, Miss Murray?'

They got into the car and she explained. 'It was in Castlemore, just as I turned into the main road. A van bumped into me. It hardly did any damage and I wanted to ignore it, but there was a policeman there and he insisted on taking down the particulars. Oh, it went on and on. I thought I was never going to get away.'

Fallon chuckled. 'There you are. I warned you about the unexpected, didn't I?'

She sighed and leaned back against the seat. 'Well, what's the next move?' He told her about the situation on the border into

Donegall and then about Hannah Costello
and her farm in the Sperrins. She was quiet
for a moment when he had finished and finally
said, 'Well, it seems like a good idea. There
doesn't appear to be much else we can do.'

'That's true,' he said. 'Anyway, we'll get
moving. I'll drive. I know the country well
from here.'

They changed places and Murphy sat in
the back. As Fallon switched on the ignition,
rain began to patter against the windscreen
and he cursed softly. He drove at a moderate
pace through a maze of narrow country
back roads, moving steadily away from
Stramore all the time. Within the first hour
Anne Murray and the boy had fallen asleep.
The rain increased into a heavy downpour
that drummed on the roof like hailstones.
Fallon's eyes began to tire. Once the lids
dropped over them and he had to jerk the
wheel over hard to keep the car out of a ditch.
The rain seemed to be getting worse and the
windscreen wipers were beginning to prove
inadequate. The headlights picked out a
narrow track that disappeared into a wood

on the left and he slowed down and swung the car into it. He cut the engine when the car was under the shelter of the trees and pulling up his collar, he settled down into the seat and went to sleep.

When he awoke he was stiff and cramped. Anne Murray's head was pillowed on his shoulder and he gently pushed her over into her own seat. The clock on the dash-board showed the time as a quarter-to-four. He started up the engine and backed the car into the road without waking the other two.

The rain had almost stopped and he felt curiously refreshed and alert. The road began to lift before him and the engine took on a deeper note as it started to pull strongly on the hills. Gradually a faint light suffused the sky in the east. Within half an hour he could see quite clearly the bulk of the mountains rising before him.

The rain stopped and he opened the side window and drove with the wind fanning his cheek. Overhead a flight of wildfowl called to him as they lifted over the grey bald faces of the hills. The car moved on through a quiet glen and the skies slowly cleared as the sun showed through.

At about five-thirty he turned the car into a narrow, badly surfaced road that was little better than a track. There was no signpost pointing its destination. About ten minutes later the car lifted over a sudden rise and there below was a small, silent valley. Fallon braked and lit a cigarette. In the midst of a clump of old beech trees an ancient, grey-stone farmhouse was rooted into the ground. He released the handbrake and the car rolled down the steep hill into the valley. As he watched, a tall, gaunt woman stepped from a door and stood holding a bucket, one hand shading her eyes as she looked towards the descending car. Relief flooded through him. It was Hannah Costello. There was a slight groan beside him and Anne slowly awakened. She opened her eyes and stared sleepily about her. 'Where are we?' she said.

Fallon grinned. 'We're here,' he said as he turned the car off the track into the farmyard and cut the engine.

9

The wind rushed through the beech trees plucking most of the remaining leaves from the branches and lifting them high over the roof top. Fallon stood at the kitchen window and looked across the valley to the heather covered hillside. His eyes lifted to where the mountain tops touched the sky and a tiny smile tugged at the corners of his mouth. He felt completely relaxed and at peace. There was a sound behind him and he turned round. Hannah Costello came into the room. 'A nice girl yon,' she said simply.

He nodded. 'What have you done with her?'

'I've put her in my bed,' Hannah said. 'The poor young creature's all in.'

He moved across to the table. 'She's not used to the life.'

'And how would she be and her a decent young woman?' Hannah said fiercely as she broke eggs into a frying pan.

Murphy came in, his face shining and his hair tousled and damp. 'What a place, Mr Fallon,' he said enthusiastically. 'Peace and quiet – and the air. I've never tasted anything like it.'

Hannah Costello lifted the eggs on to two plates and put them on the table. 'There, get that inside you,' she said. 'There's plenty of bread and jam, if you're still hungry afterwards.'

Murphy eagerly started eating. He swallowed the first mouthful and said gaily, 'Marvellous! You've got the touch all right, Mrs Costello.'

She snorted. 'None of your blarney here. You'll pay for it whether you like it or not.' She picked up two buckets and turned a forbidding look on Fallon. 'I'll be in the cow byre. I want to see you when you've finished your breakfast.'

When she had gone Murphy grimaced. 'What a woman, Mr Fallon. Never the soft word from that one.'

Fallon smiled. 'You'll soon find out that she is soft,' he said. 'Oh, she'll charge us for everything we have, but she'll do anything she can to help. She's a good woman. I wonder what happened to those two sons of hers.'

Murphy grinned. 'The appetite this place gives you she probably couldn't afford to feed them any longer.'

Fallon smiled, swallowed a cup of tea, and went out into the bright morning. Two or three white clouds scudded across a blue sky and the warmth of the sun touched his face. He sauntered across to the cow byre and went in. His nose wrinkled with delight at the old, familiar smell of animals and straw. He chuckled and said, 'There's nothing quite like the smell of a cow byre.'

Hannah Costello was sitting on a stool milking. She smiled over her shoulder and said, 'You know what they say – once a farm boy always a farm boy.'

231

He moved across and leaned on the stall beside her. 'There's something in that,' he said. 'Country pleasures are the only ones.'

She laughed grimly. 'Aye, on a day like this with white clouds and a blue sky but come up here in January. You'd soon change your mind.'

He laughed lightly. 'Perhaps you're right.' He watched her for a moment and then said, 'What's happened to the boys?'

Her shoulders dipped rhythmically as her hands worked. She stood up and moved to the next cow. 'James is dead,' she said. Her voice was quite flat and unemotional.

'What happened?' Fallon said in surprise.

She sighed. 'He got tired of the farm. Fancied going adventuring. He joined the Ulster Rifles. He was killed somewhere in Korea. I never could remember the name of the place.'

'There was another, wasn't there?' Fallon said. 'A younger one?'

She nodded. 'You mean Charlie – he's still here. He's eighteen now.'

Fallon frowned in puzzlement. 'Where is he? He must have been out early.'

She finished milking the cow and sat back on the stool. 'He didn't come home last night,' she said. 'He does that often. Spends the night on the hillside watching the stars or some such foolishness.' She stood up and said briskly, 'He took bad with the meningitis when he was thirteen. His wits are clean gone.' Fallon couldn't think of anything to say. She gazed at him quizzically. 'You aren't by any chance feeling sorry for me are you?'

He smiled and reached for the milk pail. 'Well almost,' he said.

She slapped his hand. 'Put that damned pail down. I'm not decrepit yet.' She leaned against the stall. 'Now give me a cigarette and tell me what you've been up to. I haven't seen a paper in a week.'

He told her everything from the very beginning – from the night O'Hara and Doolan had arrived at his cottage. When he had finished there was a long silence. After a while he shifted uncomfortably and said, 'What do you think?'

She grunted scornfully. 'I think you're the biggest bloody fool in the world,' she said.

'That's what I think.' She shook her head. 'The one thing I can't forgive is the way you've involved that poor girl. You've ruined her.'

He nodded his head several times and kicked viciously at the side of the stall. 'I know. I know. But there was a sort of inevitability about that. And anyway,' he added defensively, 'she's absolutely in the clear as long as Rogan keeps his mouth shut. The trouble is, I think he'll spill his guts if the police get their hands on him.'

She picked up the pail and he followed her from the byre. 'I know Rogan,' she said. 'He stayed here last year. He's a bad one. The worst I've ever come across.'

Fallon sighed. 'I don't know where they found him. He's a fine example of the Irish patriot, I must say.'

She laughed coldly. 'The Organization has to take what it can get these days and that's the truth of it. They aren't getting the educated idealists like they used to. They have to recruit from the scum who'd have ended up on the wrong side of the law anyway.'

'It was different in the old days,' he said wistfully.

She turned on him, suddenly stormy. 'Of course it was,' she said. 'But times have changed. You're an anachronism. You're out of date – old fashioned.' She shook her head sorrowfully. 'You should never have come back.'

He took a deep breath and managed a smile. 'I'm beginning to realize that.' For a moment he stood silently, kicking at the ground with the toe of his shoe and then he said, 'I think I'll go for a walk. If young Murphy tries to follow me head him off will you? I'd like to be on my own.' She nodded sombrely and he turned on heel and cut across the yard and out of the gate.

At the back of the farmhouse there was a small glen slanting back into the hills and he plunged into it, scrambling over a jumbled mass of great boulders and stones.

The glen lifted a little and the boulders gave way to thick heather and springy moss. A small stream rattled over white stones and he stood listening to it for a while and then a cloud drifted across the face of the sun and a shadow fell across that place. The sound of the stream faded into the background and there was only the silence. Fallon turned deadly cold and a thrill of elemental fear moved inside him. Here in this quiet glen he was face to face with the silence of eternity and he suddenly realized his own insignificance in the general scheme of things.

He stood as if turned to stone, hardly daring to breathe, and then the sound of the stream gradually came back to him and a small breeze rustled through the heather. He took out his handkerchief and wiped the beads of perspiration from his brow. When he sat down on the springy turf and put a cigarette in his mouth, his hands trembled slightly. He drew the smoke deep into his lungs and after a while he felt better. He stretched out on his back and narrowed his eyes against the brightness of the sky.

He began to think about Anne Murray. Hannah had been right, of course. Anything that had happened to the girl was entirely his fault. He should never have gone back to her house on that fatal night. When he considered things logically everything that had happened was his fault because everything could be traced back to Rogan and he was the one who had set Rogan free. He realized one thing very clearly. Anne Murray would have to go. The only trouble would be in persuading her that such a course was sensible. He sighed and closed his eyes and his sigh merged with the breeze and the soughing of the heather and the rattle of the water over the stones and he slept.

When he opened his eyes Anne Murray was sitting by his side gazing pensively into the stream, lost in some dream world of her own. He lay quietly watching her for a while and suddenly, with a sense of wonder, he realized that she was beautiful. He stirred and sat up. She turned quickly and a smile appeared on her face. She glowed as if a lamp had been turned on inside her. 'How do you feel?' she said.

He smiled gravely. 'Not so bad. How long have you been here?'

She shrugged. 'About half an hour. You haven't been sleeping for very long. Hannah told me you'd come up this way. She said she thought you needed me.'

He nodded slowly. 'I see. That was considerate of her.'

'Don't be bitter,' she said. 'It doesn't suit you. She's a good woman. I like her and what's more, she likes you – very much.'

'They always do,' he said. 'Even my mother thought I was the darlin' boy.' He took out his cigarettes and offered her one and she shook her head.

'What's got into you?' she asked. 'There's a bitterness in you at the moment. That's something I haven't noticed before.'

He smiled apologetically. 'Wormwood and gall. I'm not very proud of myself at the moment.'

'I see.' She nodded slowly. 'Any particular reason?'

He shrugged. 'Lots of reasons. Nearly everything that's happened during the last few days is my fault.'

'Rogan's!' she interrupted.

He shook his head. 'Mine! After all, I was the one that set him free.'

She laughed in a peculiar way and shook her head. 'And I thought you were intelligent.'

A tiny flicker of anger moved in him. 'Don't you think I am now?'

She shrugged and said warmly, 'Then start thinking like an intelligent person. You're blaming yourself for what Rogan's done. All right – you set him free. I'll grant you that, but where does anything begin? Do you know? I'm sure I don't. What made Rogan what he was? What started him along his chosen path? Are you to blame for that?' She shook her head and said slowly, 'If it comes to that, what started *you* off in this game?'

He threw pebbles into the stream in an abstracted manner as he replied. 'Something deep down in the depths of childhood. A bright dream. Banners and heroes and the old tales. Charles Stuart Parnell and Wolfe Tone.' He sighed. 'Most men grow out of things like that – I never did, that's all.'

She shook her head. 'No, it's something more than that. Something that's inherent in the Gael. A sort of agonized eternal struggle inside that moves him towards self-destruction.'

For a moment he remained sitting on the ground staring into the stream thinking about what she had said and then he jumped up and laughed gaily. 'For God's sake let's forget about it all, for an hour or two at least.' He reached out a hand and pulled her up. 'Look around you at the hills and the sun and the heather. It's a perfect day and it's ours to do with as we please.'

The colour swept into her cheeks and she laughed and pushed back her hair, blown by the wind. 'All right,' she said. 'What shall we do?'

'Climb to the top of the mountain,' he said. 'We've just got time before dinner.' He grabbed her hand and they started to scramble up the glen side.

It was not a very high mountain but when they came out on top of it she caught her breath and gave a deep sigh of contentment. 'It's lovely,' she said. 'I've never seen anything so beautiful.'

Fallon gazed out over the mountainside and nodded. It *was* beautiful but not in the

way that she was. He stood slightly behind
her and watched her wistfully. The wind
folded her skirt about her legs outlining the
long clean sweep of her limbs and her golden
hair sparkled in the sun. She fitted perfectly
into the scene. A golden girl in a golden day
and a terrible sadness swept over him because
he knew that this day was a special gift from
fate. A short breathing space before the darkness closed in finally.

He pulled himself together and let the wind
blow his black thoughts away. Today was
theirs and he was going to damn well enjoy
every minute of it. He reached out and took
her hand in his and cried, 'Come on!' and
plunged down the mountainside.

Anne Murray was shrieking with delight
as they rushed downwards, stumbling over
the tussocks, never stopping until they were
once more in the small glen by the stream.
She collapsed against Fallon breathless and
laughing. He held her lightly in his arms for
a moment and then she looked over his
shoulder and her eyes widened. He turned
quickly. Standing knee-deep in the heather on

the opposite side of the stream was a youth. He was tall and thin with long hair and bowed shoulders and there was a vacant expression on his face. He smiled and leapt across the stream with one agile bound and came towards them. He carried a canvas sleeping-bag under one arm and a dead rabbit swung from his other hand. Anne stepped back in alarm and Fallon tightened his arm about her shoulders. 'Don't be alarmed. This will be Hannah's son – Charlie.'

The boy stood a few paces away from them and held up the dead rabbit. 'I found it,' he said. 'A stoat had him but I chased him away.' He looked at the rabbit and said sorrowfully, 'He's dead.'

Fallon smiled. 'What are you going to do with him. Have him for dinner?'

An expression of indignation flashed across Charlie's face. 'I'm going to bury him. I always bury them.'

Anne moved nervously and Fallon whispered, 'Don't worry. He's absolutely harmless.' He raised his voice and said, 'Did you have a good night?'

Charlie smiled and nodded. 'I slept in the old shooting hut on the other side of the mountain and when the rain stopped I went outside. The stars were lovely – like diamonds sparkling in the sky – thousands of them.' There was an expression of ecstasy on his face.

Fallon squeezed Anne's hand reassuringly and said, 'We're going down to the farm now. Are you going to come with us?'

Charlie smiled eagerly. 'I'd like that. I like it when we have people staying. We haven't had anybody staying for a long time now.'

As they went down the glen towards the farm he walked beside them, sometimes running a little distance away to look at something, like a child. He talked constantly about the birds and the animals that lived on the hillside as if they were personal friends. 'What happened to him?' Anne whispered to Fallon at one point. He explained about the boy's illness and compassion appeared on her face. 'How terrible. I've come across one or two cases like it during my hospital work. It's one of the most depressing things a doctor can handle. There's so very little that can be done.'

Fallon nodded. 'He looks happy enough,' he said and then sighed. 'Life can be inexpressibly cruel when it wants to be.'

They crossed the farmyard and entered the kitchen to find the table laid and Hannah fuming at the stove. 'You nearly missed your dinner,' she said. 'We were just going to start.'

Murphy was sitting at the table and he winked across at Fallon and Anne and said, 'I hope your walk has sharpened your appetites.'

Anne blushed and sat down quickly and Hannah turned to her son and said, 'Now then, Charlie. Leave that rabbit outside and wash your hands. You can't have your dinner until you do.'

It was a gay meal and Johnny Murphy kept up a constant barrage of conversation, chiefly directed towards Hannah. Gradually the old woman unbent and once or twice a smile flashed across her seamed, weather-beaten face. When the meal was over Anne moved across to the sink and offered to help with the dishes. Hannah scowled. 'Not while you're a guest here,' she said. 'A paying guest at that. If you've got any sense you'll take to the hills for the afternoon, the lot of you. I'll give you some sandwiches. Charlie can guide you.' She looked out of the window at the sky and said, 'The rain will be back tonight. This is the last fine day we'll get before the winter.'

Anne turned to Fallon, an eager smile on her face, and Johnny Murphy jumped up enthusiastically. 'It's a grand idea, Mr Fallon. Let's go.'

For a moment Fallon hesitated and then he remembered that quiet moment on the mountain when he had realized that this day was to be the only one and he slammed his hand down on the table. 'All right then, what are we waiting for?'

Twenty minutes later they were striding up the glen away from the farmhouse, cutting deep into the hills. It was the happiest afternoon Fallon could ever remember. Murphy and Charlie walked together, leading the way, and he and Anne brought up the rear.

The air was like wine and the sun was warm on their backs. When they reached the top of the mountain it was as though they were on top of the world and all the fear and the violence of the past few days was left behind them.

They had their sandwiches in the shooting hut that Charlie had mentioned and then carried on across a wide moor, purple with heather and sweet smelling. In the late afternoon they came back over the mountain and stood on the top looking down over the valley for the last time. A faint breeze lifted over the hills and in the east the sky was beginning to darken. Fallon stood gazing down into the little glen and it was so still he could just hear the sound of the water as it splashed over the stones in the stream bed. Anne Murray stirred beside him and said in a voice that was infinitely sad, 'I wish this day could go on for ever.'

He wanted to make some suitable reply, but there was nothing he could say. Nothing that would give her the comfort she needed. He gently took her hand in his and squeezed it and they moved down the hillside, back towards the farm.

The rain came later that evening when Fallon strolled alone through the farmyard after supper. The air was heavy and still and the rain started with a sudden heavy rush as if it wanted to take everyone by surprise. He ran quickly to the old barn that stood nearby and wrenched open the door. There was a ladder that slanted up to a loft and he climbed it and sat in the sweet-smelling hay next to a round window and stared out into the rain. There was a slight creaking as someone came up the ladder and then a form moved through the darkness and sat down opposite him. 'I saw you run in here,' Anne Murray said. 'I've brought you your raincoat.'

He reached out through the darkness and took the coat from her. Their fingers touched. For a moment they sat there breathless and waiting in the darkness and then she lurched forward into his arms. 'Oh, Martin. I love you. I love you so very much.' She repeated his name over and over again, breathlessly.

He held her close, her head pillowed

against his breast, and after a while he said sadly, 'This might have meant something to me a long time ago.'

'Then why not now?' she demanded fiercely.

He smiled. 'Because I'm too old – and I don't mean just in years. Because I destroyed myself a long time ago.' He pushed her away from him and gripped her arms savagely. 'Can't you see that I'm just a dead man walking? I have been since the day I joined the Organization.'

She pushed her arms about his neck and kissed him; fierce bruising kisses that burned down into his very being and sent his senses reeling. For a moment he gave in. His arms crushed her and he returned her kisses avidly, but there was still that small core of reason burning within him that told him it was useless.

He pushed her away from him and said urgently, 'There's no hope for us – can't you understand that? No hope at all.'

She went very still. After a while she said, 'But what about your cottage across the border – no one can touch us there.'

He shook his head and sighed. 'Except me,'

he said. 'Even if we made it there would always be the emptiness in me.' He stared out into the rain. 'I've destroyed myself. I'm damned if I'm going to destroy you.'

She pushed herself back on her knees and said evenly, 'I see. And what if I told you I wasn't going to take any notice of you.'

He shrugged. 'You'll have to, because at the first available opportunity we're going to part company.' She started to speak and he raised his voice and went on. 'No ifs or buts. You're going to buy a train ticket and you're going to cross the border. You'll be safe over there until this Rogan business is settled. After all, you'll be able to cross over easily enough. They aren't looking for you yet.'

'And how do you propose to make me do all this?' she said quietly.

He shrugged. 'We're going to part company whether you like it or not.' There was a grim finality in his voice.

For a long time there was a silence and then she raised her head and he saw the white blur of her face through the darkness. She was perfectly calm when she spoke. 'Whatever happens I shall go to that cottage in Cavan. Always remember that.'

For a moment the love leaped up inside him and he moved towards her, his hands trembling, and then with a sudden roar, headlights lifted over the hill and came down the dirt road towards the farm. Fallon got to his feet and stared out into the rain. A small van turned in through the gates and bumped across the yard towards the farm. As he watched, the door opened and Hannah Costello stood framed in the light. A figure got out of the van and moved towards her. For a moment they stood talking and then they both went in and the door was closed.

The girl gripped his arm tightly. 'Who do you think it is?' she said and there was fear in her voice.

He shrugged and moved towards the ladder. 'Could be anybody.' He quickly descended the ladder and held it steady as she followed him. She handed him his trenchcoat and he draped it across his shoulders and said, 'We'd better go and find out.' He took her hand and together they ran through the heavy rain to the farm door.

For a moment they paused outside the door. Inside they could hear voices and suddenly Johnny Murphy shouted, 'I'll kill you, you dirty bastard.'

Fallon flung open the door and stepped into the room. Hannah was standing by the fire, an expression of grim determination on her face and Murphy crouched by the table, a poker held in one hand. Patrick Rogan was standing facing them.

Fallon stepped forward and his trenchcoat fell to the floor. Rogan turned, a look of alarm on his face that he quickly erased with a smile. 'Is it yourself, Mr Fallon?' he said. 'I'm glad to see you all made it safely.'

Fallon paused three paces away from him. 'What do you want here, Rogan?' he said in an ice-calm voice.

Rogan shrugged and said nervously, 'The terrible time I've had of it – you'd never believe. I left Castlemore on top of a cattle truck. Friends gave me shelter in a village near Stramore for a few days but the search is that fierce now, they panicked.' He shook his head. 'They turned me out, Mr Fallon. Did you ever hear the like of that?'

'They probably liked you about as much as we do,' Murphy said.

Rogan ignored the remark. His cheeks were hollow and unshaven and his right eyelid twitched nervously. 'I pinched that van in Stramore,' he said. 'I knew I'd be safe if I could get here.'

Hannah grunted and swept across the room to the kitchen sink where she began to dry some plates rapidly. 'You can get out,' she said. 'I've told you once. I wouldn't cut you down if you were hanging.'

Rogan turned on her. 'For God's sake, Hannah. You wouldn't turn a dog out on a night like this.'

'I like dogs,' she said calmly. 'Now get out, you butcher.'

'He isn't going anywhere,' Fallon said. 'He's going to get what he deserves.'

He took one step forward and Anne Murray screamed high and clear, 'No, Martin! No!' And then Rogan jumped back, sudden fury on his face, and pulled a revolver out of his raincoat pocket.

Fallon grabbed for the wrist and deflected the weapon so that the bullet went into the floor. For a moment they swayed together and then he managed to get purchase and twisted and threw the small man over his hip. Rogan crashed heavily to the floor and Fallon kicked the revolver from his hand. As he moved forward Rogan grabbed at his legs and pulled and Fallon fell against the table. The small man scrambled to his feet and moved in. His right fist thudded home under Fallon's ribs and a terrible pain flared through his wound causing him to half scream. In his agony he lashed out blindly and his fist caught Rogan in the mouth. He went flying across the room and crashed into the door and Fallon lurched after him and hit him again. Rogan began to slide down the wall, a glazed look in his eyes, and Fallon held him by the coat and began to hit him in the face, the blows thudding home mercilessly.

He could hear confused babbling of sound behind him and Anne Murray was screaming and then hands wrenched him away and he was staring down the twin barrels of a shotgun that was firmly grasped in Hannah Costello's hands. She thumbed back the hammers and said grimly, 'If you make another move I'll blast you, Martin.'

Fallon turned and leaned on the table gasping for breath and Hannah wrenched open the door and said to Rogan, 'Go on, get out of it while you're still in one piece.'

Rogan staggered to the doorway. For a moment he leaned there and then he said in tones of the utmost malevolence, 'I'm going to kill you, Fallon. I swear it. Somehow, somewhere I'll catch up with you.' He lurched into the night and Hannah closed the door. A moment later the van bumped across the yard and out into the road and the sound of its engine faded away into the night.

Hannah walked over to a cupboard and put the shotgun away. She said calmly, 'I wasn't going to have you kill him, Martin. He isn't worth it.'

For a moment Fallon stayed leaning heavily on the table and then he stood up and moved across to the far door. 'I think I'll go to bed,' he said in a steady voice. He staggered against the door, clutching for support, and Murphy moved quickly to aid him. Fallon pushed him away and turned to face them. 'We'll have to leave first thing in the morning,' he said. 'We can't stay now. There's no telling what Rogan might do.' He looked across at Anne Murray who was standing by the table looking somehow forlorn and alone. 'And you'll catch that train in Stramore tomorrow,' he said.

For a moment it seemed as if she was going to speak and then she suddenly sat down at the table and burst into tears. For a little while Fallon stood looking at her, a great pity in his heart, and then he opened the door and quietly left the room.

10

Fallon shared a bed with Murphy but his wound pained him and what little sleep he did manage to get, was disturbed and full of bad dreams. He lay in that empty world between sleeping and waking and stared at the ceiling. It had stopped raining and a white band of moonlight sprawled across the bed. He lit a cigarette and glanced at his watch. It was almost two o'clock. He lay back against the pillow, his whole body wet with perspiration, and on a sudden impulse, lifted the blankets aside and slipped out of bed.

He quickly dried his body on a towel and dressed. Murphy was sleeping peacefully, his breathing steady and regular. Fallon crept stealthily across to the door and opened it gently. The corridor was dark and quiet with an irregular patch of light on the floor at the far end where the moon showed through the window. He moved quietly along to the stairs and then froze as he heard a door click open in the kitchen.

For a moment Fallon didn't move, his ears strained for the slightest sound, and then he went cautiously downstairs and paused outside the kitchen door listening. There was no sound. He turned the knob carefully and flung the door open and stepped quickly into the room. There was no one there.

For a moment he stood there, a puzzled frown on his face, and then he heard the click of the outside door. He passed quickly to the window and was just in time to see Charlie crossing the yard in the bright moonlight. He was carrying the shotgun over one shoulder.

Fallon relaxed and reached for a cigarette and then there was a sound behind him. He turned to find Hannah holding a lamp standing in the doorway. She was in her nightclothes and Anne was at her shoulder. 'What's going on here?' Hannah said.

Fallon smiled as she came forward and put the lamp down on the table. 'It's all right,' he said. 'I heard a noise down here. I thought it might be our friend returning so I came down to investigate. It was only Charlie. I saw him crossing the yard. I wondered where he'd disappeared to when he didn't show up for supper.'

Hannah raised a hand and said, 'God knows where he gets to – I'm sure I don't. He comes and goes throughout the night. I leave him to please himself, poor lad.'

Anne sat down on a chair by the table. 'I'm glad it was only Charlie,' she said. 'I was scared stiff when I heard that door crash open.'

'And so was I.' Murphy appeared in the doorway. He yawned and scratched his head. 'Is everything all right, Mr Fallon?'

Fallon nodded. 'Only Charlie up to his usual nocturnal tricks, prowling off into the night with a shotgun. Going to do a bit of poaching I expect.'

Hannah was filling the kettle at the sink. She turned quickly. 'Did you say he had the shotgun?'

Fallon nodded. 'That's right – carried it over his shoulder. I saw it distinctly in the moonlight.'

She moved across to the cupboard and opened it quickly. 'That's funny,' she said slowly. 'He's taken a box of cartridges as well.'

There was a little moment of silence and Fallon said, 'What's so unusual about that?'

'I don't let him use the shotgun at all,' Hannah Costello said. 'It's a strict rule. He never touches it.'

Fallon had been leaning against the wall. He straightened up and took a pace forward and then the door was kicked open and a voice cried, 'Stand where you are – everybody!'

Rogan stood just inside the door holding the shotgun at his waist. The barrels were shaking slightly and he was trembling. Fallon took the beginnings of a step towards him and Rogan said sharply, 'Stay where you are.

I've only got to press these triggers and you'll get both barrels and that's enough to finish the lot of you off.'

Fallon's throat had suddenly gone dry. 'What do you want, Rogan?' he said.

The small man's lips curled back from his teeth. 'I'm going to kill you, Fallon.' A slight line of froth began to appear on his lips and he giggled, high-pitched and horrible, like an old woman. 'I'm going to stand you against the wall and I'm going to give you both barrels in the belly. How does that sound?'

'You're mad!' Anne Murray said in horror. 'You're out your mind, Rogan.'

She took a quick step towards him and Fallon shouted, 'Stay where you are, Anne! Don't move.'

At that moment Charlie appeared in the doorway behind Rogan. There was a big grin on his face and he laughed and said, 'Are we playing the game now, Mr Rogan? Is this the game?'

Rogan spoke without turning round. 'Come in here, Charlie, and go and stand by your mother.' He giggled again. 'I met Charlie along the road after you threw me out. We had a nice chat, didn't we Charlie? I asked him to get me the shotgun so we could have some fun – play a little joke on you all.'

He began to laugh horribly and Charlie laughed with him. He shambled closer to Rogan and said, 'Let me hold it for a while, Mr Rogan,' and reached for the shotgun.

'Get away!' Rogan snarled. Charlie's smile disappeared. An uncertain expression appeared on his face. For a moment he hesitated and then he reached out towards the gun. Rogan stepped back and smashed the boy across the head with the butt, then he turned and covered the rest of them again.

Charlie slipped to the floor, moaning and clutching his head. Blood began to seep between his fingers. 'You damned swine!' Hannah said. 'I'll pay you out for that.'

Charlie crawled across the room and huddled against her skirts like a hurt dog and Rogan took another step back until he was standing in the doorway. 'This has gone on long enough. The rest of you move back against the far door and you stand against the wall, Fallon.' Anne stifled a scream in her throat and Rogan shouted, 'Go on – do as you're told!'

'Do as he tells you,' Fallon said quietly. 'Can't you see he's mad? He'll murder the lot of you if it suits him.' He began to back slowly to the wall, his eyes cast down. He was judging the distance very carefully because lying under the table, half covered by a corner of a loose rug, was the revolver he had kicked out of Rogan's hand earlier in the evening. In the excitement they had forgotten all about it.

His hand touched the wall behind him and Rogan said harshly, 'That's just right.' He started to raise the shotgun to his shoulder and Fallon dived headfirst under the table.

Anne Murray screamed piercingly and as he clawed for the revolver, Fallon knew that he was too late. There was a confused shouting and Murphy cried, 'Save yourself, Mr Fallon!' as he had done on another occasion, and jumped up on the table and threw himself at Rogan.

Rogan stepped backwards and fired one

barrel. The blast caught Murphy in the stomach and chest at point blank range and he screamed and twisted in mid-air and landed heavily on the floor.

Fallon took a snap shot with the revolver as he rolled on his stomach and wood splinters flew from the door post at the side of Rogan's head. He turned and vanished into the night.

Fallon didn't wait for anything. There was only one thought driving through his brain. He had to kill Rogan. He went through the door like a fury and fired once at the stumbling figure of his enemy as he crossed the yard. Rogan whirled and fired the other barrel of the shotgun and Fallon dropped flat on his face, the shot whistling over his head. Rogan ran into the cow byre and Fallon, crouching low, crossed the yard, and threw himself down by the entrance.

Inside the cows were moving uneasily. There was a rattle of chains and the door at the far end swung open. Fallon cautiously peered round the door and said, 'I'm going to kill you, Rogan, so don't lose your nerve and come

out with your hands up. Any way you come,
I'm going to put a bullet through you.'

There was no reply. The cows began to
trample about in their stalls and Fallon
waited. The shotgun went off with a thun-
derous roar, and lead shot hummed through
the entrance. Immediately Fallon jumped
inside and dived for the nearest stall. The
shotgun blasted again and he rolled and fired
hastily as Rogan ducked through the entrance
at the other end of the building and disappeared from sight.

Fallon scrambled to his feet and ran out
of the door. He crossed the yard, his head
down and the revolver ready, and turned the
corner of the barn in time to catch Rogan
crossing the open field towards the road. He
took careful aim and fired. Rogan ignored
the shot. He scrambled over the fence and
started to run down the road.

Fallon ran after him. Before he had gone
fifty yards he was in trouble. The old agony
flared up in his side and each breath he took
sent a stab of jagged pain coursing through
him. The sweat poured from his brow, but

he clenched his teeth and kept going. He laboured up a little hill and a fast moving cloud passed across the face of the moon and darkness descended on the road. He paused on top of the hill and crouched low, his eyes searching the darkness, and then some sixth sense caused him to drop flat on his face.

Shot whined through the air above his head as Rogan fired both barrels and the echoes of the blast reverberated from the hills. Fallon fired once in the direction of the flash and scrambled wearily to his feet. At that moment the cloud passed and the moon came into view again.

Rogan was about forty yards away and a few yards beyond him, the van was parked at the side of the road. Fallon's hand was shaking. He took a deep breath and, resting the barrel of the pistol across his arm, took careful aim. He squeezed the trigger. Rogan seemed to trip. He turned a somersault on the ground and lay there twitching. Fallon shouted in triumph, but even as he started forward, Rogan got to his feet and lurched on towards the van, dragging one leg. Fallon raised the revolver and pulled the trigger. There was a harmless click. Rogan reached the van and wrenched open the door. A moment later the engine roared into life and the van began to move. Fallon gave a howl of rage and disappointment and threw the empty revolver after the fleeing vehicle. The van dipped over a hill in the road and disappeared from sight and the sound of it died into the distance.

He turned and limped back towards the farmhouse. He tried to take short breaths because he found they didn't hurt him as much. As he was passing through the gate he paused and clutched at the fence for support as a terrible burning pain coursed through his entire body. He had never experienced such agony before. He hung on for several minutes until gradually the pain died away and he could breathe easily again. He wiped the perspiration from his face with a handkerchief and his hands were shaking. There was something wrong. Something very wrong. He knew it was the wound – there was nothing else it could be. For the moment, however, the only thing that interested him was what had happened to Murphy.

He opened the door and stepped into the kitchen. Anne Murray was standing with her back to him, her arms bared to the elbows and covered with blood. Johnny Murphy was lying on the table staring up at the ceiling. Hannah was wiping the sweat from his forehead with a damp cloth. Every now and then his eyes rolled up and he stifled a scream in his throat. Fallon moved over to the table and looked down. The boy's stomach was like a piece of raw meat and there was more blood than Fallon had ever seen in his life before. He closed his eyes and turned away. 'Holy Mother of God!' he said.

The girl was attempting to block some of the more serious gashes with great pads of lint and cotton wool. 'We'll have to get him to a hospital,' she said.

'The nearest one's Stramore,' Hannah told her.

There was a moment of absolute stillness as Anne Murray's back stiffened and then the boy groaned deeply and she returned to her bandaging. 'We'll have to try,' she said.

Fallon took a deep breath and walked forward until he was standing at the side of the table looking down at the boy. Murphy opened his eyes and death stared out at Fallon. The boy struggled for words and Fallon said, 'Don't try to speak. We'll get you to a doctor. You're going to be all right.'

Murphy shook his head weakly and a tired grin touched the corners of his mouth. 'The terrible liar you are, Mr Fallon.' He closed his eyes for a moment and then opened them again. 'Did you get him?' he said with difficulty.

For a moment Fallon hesitated and then he smiled and took one of the boy's hands in his. 'Yes. I got him,' he said.

A smile of deep content appeared on the white face and Murphy closed his eyes. 'Up the Republic, Mr Fallon!' he said. His hand tightened on Fallon's for a moment and then it slackened and his head turned gently to one side.

Over in the corner Charlie was crying

quietly. For a little while Fallon stood staring down at the body and then he turned away wearily and went to the window. 'Did you get him?' Hannah said quietly.

He shook his head. 'No, I winged him, but he managed to get to his van. He's ten miles away by now.'

He sank down in a chair and dropped his head into his hands. Hannah moved over to him and patted him on the shoulder. 'Don't blame yourself, Martin,' she said. 'It was meant to be. None of us can argue with fate.'

He looked up at her and smiled tightly. 'But I do blame myself – that's the trouble.'

She frowned and raised her eyebrows. 'Then blame yourself if it makes you happy. The boy gave his life to save you – don't throw it back in his face by wasting it.' She moved across to Charlie and shook him. 'Come on, get up. Go and get two spades from the tool shed.' Charlie left the room, snivelling, and Hannah said to Fallon, 'I want him buried and out of the way before morning.'

He nodded and stood up wearily. Anne

Murray was washing her arms under the tap. When she turned to dry them he saw that her face was set and white. 'Are you all right?' he said.

She nodded and said in a controlled voice, 'Perfectly. I'll help Hannah sew him up in a blanket while you dig the grave.' She moved across to the table and started to straighten the limbs. Fallon looked at her in amazement and then went slowly outside.

They dug the grave at the back of the farm just where the little glen began to lift back into the hills. Charlie was still sobbing intermittently and Fallon ignored him and dug mechanically. His mind was frozen by the shock of Murphy's death. He realized how very much the boy had come to mean to him during the past few days. He dug his spade viciously into the soil and wished bitterly that he had refused to allow the boy to become involved in the beginning.

When the hole was deep enough they went back to the house for the body. It was lying on the table, a shapeless bundle in a blanket, and Charlie brought in a plank.

271

They placed the body on the plank and he and Fallon carried it up the slope behind the farmhouse and the two women followed. They lowered the body down into the hole and gently laid it on the bottom. Fallon coughed and said, 'Does anybody know anything to say?'

There was a silence and then Hannah Costello said in a hard voice, 'There's only one thing to say – Here lies a fine young boy whose life was wasted – his only memorial, the stupidity of men.' She turned to her son and said, 'Charlie, fill the hole in,' and then she took Anne Murray by the arm and gently led her away.

Fallon stood for a long time looking down at the grave and then he lifted his eyes up to the stars. It was utterly still and somewhere, miles away in the distance, a dog barked. He felt more alone than he had ever been in his life and he shivered and turned and went down to the farm.

They left shortly before six. Fallon went into the kitchen to settle-up with Hannah, but when she saw his wallet she held up a hand. 'Not this time,' she said. 'I'm not that much of a vulture.'

He hesitated and then put the wallet away. 'I'm sorry, Hannah,' he said. 'I seem to get everybody involved in trouble. I must be tainted.'

She snorted and wiped her hands on her apron. 'You're full of self pity, that's your trouble. If you want to pay me you can do it easily enough. Get that girl to a railway station and then leave her alone.' She gazed steadily into his eyes. 'You aren't any use to her, Martin. You've nothing to offer. Give her a chance.'

For a moment he stared fixedly at her and then he smiled. 'I will,' he said. 'I promise you I will.'

As he turned to the door, that terrible pain blossmed in his body again, filling him with fire. He reeled and clutched at the wall and Hannah rushed forward and supported him. 'What is it?' she demanded. His face was twisted in agony and she said in a whisper, 'Why, you're ill – really ill.'

He leaned on her for a moment and the

pain passed. 'I'll be all right.' He managed a smile. 'It's this wound of mine, but it's nothing.' He gripped her arm firmly and added, 'Don't tell Anne anything about it. It's going to be tough enough to get rid of her without her thinking I'm ill.'

Hannah nodded slowly and they went out to the car. Anne Murray was sitting huddled in the passenger seat and Fallon slid behind the wheel and pressed the starter. The engine picked up strongly and Hannah shouted, 'God bless you!' He released the handbrake and they moved away.

It was a fine morning with a clear sky and the sun was beginning to lift above the horizon. He drove in silence for half an hour and then the girl spoke. 'Where are we going?'

He took out his cigarettes. There was one left and he put it in his mouth and tossed the empty packet out of the window. 'We're going to Stramore,' he said. 'You're going to catch that train.'

She turned towards him and said calmly, 'I'm not catching any train. I'm sticking with you.'

'That's out of the question now,' he said. 'Surely you can see that.'

She shook her head. 'I can only see that I love you.' She squeezed his arm. 'I don't blame you for what happened to Johnny. It was tragic, it was horrible, but it wasn't your fault.'

He smiled slightly. 'Everyone's so anxious to tell me that it wasn't my fault. It's beginning to make me feel a bit suspicious.' He shook his head and said decidedly, 'The boy's death has nothing to do with it. Let's just say I don't want the responsibility of carting you around with me.'

She reached across and switched off the ignition and the car lost speed and slowed to a halt. Fallon applied the handbrake and she said, 'There's only one thing of importance at the moment. The fact that we love each other.' He didn't say anything and she said desperately, 'You do love me, don't you?' He sat silently in his seat and made no reply and then she started to cry. He sat there for several minutes, fighting the impulse to take her in his arms and comfort her, and then he started up the car and drove away.

After several minutes she stopped crying and dried her eyes. 'You do love me,' she said. 'But you're afraid of love. You've never learned how to accept.' He remained silent and she added with a sudden burst of anger, 'I'm not leaving you and that's definite.'

At that moment they turned into the main road to Stramore. There was a garage and cafe on one side and he slowed the car down and turned it into the parking space. 'Would you like anything?' he said. She shook her head. He climbed out of the car and shut the door. 'I shan't be long,' he said. 'I'm just going to the men's room.'

She nodded and tried to smile. 'All right!'

He looked in through the window and smiled. 'Cheer up! Things are never as bad as we think.'

He walked rapidly away from the car towards the cafe. He paused for a moment to insert a coin in a cigarette machine and then he went to the rear of the building. He quickly skirted the back of the cafe and moved round until he was standing hidden behind the far corner of the garage. The car was some distance away from him and he could see her head faintly through the window. A few feet away from him there was a large, covered lorry and on the side of it was painted: A. Malone – Market Gardener – Stramore. The driver climbed up into the cab of the vehicle and started the engine. Fallon glanced quickly around and could see no one. He pulled his hat down firmly and running up behind the vehicle, scrambled over the tailboard.

As the lorry paused at the edge of the road he peered over the tailboard and looked at the car for the last time. She was still sitting there, waiting for him to return. The lorry moved into the road and the engine began to roar and then the garage was only a white blob in the distance. He sat down on the floor, his back to the side of the lorry. He took out a cigarette carefully and tried to light it but there was a terrible constriction in his throat. He crushed the cigarette in his fingers and buried his face in his hands.

11

Fallon sat by the tailboard immersed in his own thoughts. It was with almost a sense of shock that he realized the lorry was passing through the outskirts of Stramore. He stood up and got ready to leave the vehicle at the first opportunity. It came sooner than he had imagined. The lorry slowed as a large removal van backed slowly out of the drive of a house into the road. Fallon vaulted to the ground, crossed the road, and walked briskly along the pavement.

He had no set plan in mind. Only one thing was definite – he had to move south, and the quicker the better. He decided to try the trains. If he was lucky enough to get on board one he could be at the border within a few hours. He walked briskly towards the centre of the town, mingling with the shoppers and keeping constantly on the move.

He crossed the market square and walked up towards the station. It was then that he received his first shock. There were policemen everywhere. Wherever he looked he saw another uniform. He turned away and hurried back towards the square. He turned down a side street and began to walk rapidly. Something had happened. Something out of the ordinary.

He paused on a street corner and hesitated. He wasn't going to last five minutes on the street, that was obvious. A police constable turned the end of the street and came towards him and Fallon dived into an alley and began to run. He slowed down at the end and turned the corner into a quiet street. Again he paused, but only for a moment, because he knew there was only one place he could go. The one place in Stramore where he would be least welcome.

It took him ten minutes to get there.

The little square was quiet and there was no sign of activity in the shop with the junk-filled windows. He moved across quickly and tried to open the door. It was locked. For a moment he hesitated then he went round the front of the building into the scrap yard at the side. There was an old, rusting van standing forlornly in the middle of the yard. He moved round it and tried the back door. It opened to his touch and he stepped into the kitchen.

Rose Conroy was working at the sink. She whirled round in surprise and a look of astonishment appeared on her face. 'Holy Mother of God!' she said. 'You're back!'

He frowned. 'I thought you were supposed to leave here.'

She dropped her gaze and said in a low voice, 'I was going to go – honest, I was, Mr Fallon. Me Dad stopped me – he found the money hidden in my room and he took it and gave me a good hiding into the bargain.' She raised hate-filled eyes. 'I'll kill him one of these days.'

Fallon shook his head. 'You won't do

anything of the sort,' he said firmly. 'He isn't worth it. Where is he at the moment?'

She shrugged. 'At the pub as usual, only this time he's spending my money.'

He grinned sympathetically. 'Never mind. I'll give you some more before I leave.'

She dried her hands on a towel. 'Why have you come back, Mr Fallon? I thought you'd have been to hell out of this by now.'

He lit a cigarette and said, 'I'm heading south on my own. I thought I'd risk the train but when I got to the station I found it crawling with peelers. What's been happening?'

She shrugged and said scornfully, 'They're looking for that fella Rogan. He was stopped in a van by a road block on the outskirts of town early this morning. He fired a shotgun out of the window and drove on.'

The room had gone strangely quiet. Fallon said, 'They haven't got him yet?'

She shook her head and laughed harshly. 'Hardly – he's upstairs now. Me Dad's furious but he's scared stiff of Rogan. He hasn't the guts to turn him away.'

It was funny how inevitable everything

was, Fallon thought. There was a pattern and when a man had an appointment with death it was impossible to avoid it. 'Is that his van outside?' he said.

She shook her head. 'That's ours.'

'I see.' He carefully stubbed out his cigarette and stood up and took off his trenchcoat. He threw it over a chair and said calmly, 'I think I'll go up and have a word with him.'

She nodded and she looked into his face, her expression changed. 'Are you all right. Mr Fallon?' she asked anxiously.

He smiled. 'I'm just a little tired,' he said. 'I'll be fine when I've had a rest.'

He passed through the living room and mounted the stairs. The corridor was very quiet and somewhere a fly buzzed against a window pane. He walked quietly along the corridor and stood listening at the door next to the girl's room. There was a faint sound of movement and a bed spring creaked. He unbuttoned his jacket and slipped his hand inside and loosened the Luger in its holster. He took a deep breath and opened the door.

Rogan was lying flat on his back under

the blankets. Fallon closed the door and leaned against it. 'Hello, you bastard!' he said, 'Isn't life full of surprises?'

Rogan sat up slowly, an expression of complete astonishment on his face. The blankets started to slide down from his shoulders and he held them in place with one hand. 'Well?' Fallon said. 'Haven't you got anything to say? I thought you were going to fix me next time we met.'

A terrible look appeared on Rogan's face and he started to laugh. Fallon's eyes narrowed. There was a bad smell here. Rogan's reactions were all wrong. He slipped his hand inside his coat and Rogan fired through the blanket. Fallon was thrown back against the wall. Oh, you fool, you bloody, stupid, dramatic fool, he thought and as his senses reeled, he was dimly aware of Rogan getting out of bed, giggling like a woman, the spittle dribbling from one corner of his mouth. Fallon wasn't conscious of taking any deliberate aim. He simply threw his arm up in a straight line and squeezed the trigger of the Luger. A black hole materialized in Rogan's head and several red marks, like cracks in a china plate, appeared like magic, running crookedly into his eyes. An expression of utter astonishment appeared on his face. He was already dead as his body flopped back on the bed.

Fallon sagged back against the door and closed his eyes. After a while he felt a little better. He grabbed hold of the door knob and pulled himself upright. For a moment or two nausea flooded through him and he leaned against the wall and breathed deeply until he recovered his senses. He walked over to the bed and looked down at the body. Rogan's eyes stared up at the ceiling and his lips were curled back from his teeth like an animal's. Fallon turned away in disgust and wrenched open the door.

The house was as quiet as when he had come in. For a moment he stood listening and then, as he approached the stairhead, the girl's voice sounded from below, 'Watch yourself, Mr Fallon. Me Dad's up there.'

As Fallon turned quickly, the door to Conroy's bedroom swung open and the old man stood revealed. He carried an iron bar in one hand and his face was flushed with drink. His little beady eyes flickered and he said, 'So you've done for him have you? But not before he gave you a touch, I see.' Fallon jerked out the Luger and then the terrible, numbing pain flooded through his body again and he cried out and doubled over.

Conroy struck the Luger from his hand with the iron bar. It was only a reflex action that made Fallon step in close and grapple with him before the old man could bring the bar down across his head.

Fallon gasped for breath and hung on grimly and gradually his senses returned. The old man was fighting mad, kicking and butting, his fingers clawing at his opponent's face. Fallon felt his back bump against the banisters at the stairhead. He dropped a shoulder and turned it up and under the old man's chin, jolting him hard. He ducked under Conroy's arm and swung him round so that he was now fighting with his back against the banister.

By now his left arm was paining him so

much it was virtually useless. He used it to block a wild punch and hit Conroy hard in the belly with his right fist. What happened next was purest accident. Conroy gulped and a fine spray of liquor erupted from his mouth as he vomited, then he lurched back against the banister. There was a splintering sound and the whole framework crashed backwards into the well of the stairs carrying Conroy with it.

Fallon stood swaying on the edge of the landing looking down at the old man. He lay with one leg twisted under him. His mouth was open and a ray of sunlight gleamed on his half-open eyes. The girl appeared and glanced up fearfully and cried out, 'For God's sake, stay where you are. You'll be breaking your neck.' Fallon moved back from the edge and she hurried up the stairs to his side and guided him downstairs.

They paused beside the body and he looked down at it and said, 'I didn't mean to kill him.'

She laughed grimly. 'The best day's work you ever did.' She gently urged him forward.

'Come on now. Into the kitchen quickly and let me have a look at you.'

She stripped his coat from him and cut his shirt off with a pair of scissors. The bullet had penetrated his left breast just below the collar bone. It was bleeding profusely. He groaned and said, 'What a bloody fool I was. I should have known from the first second that he had an ace up his sleeve. He was always frightened of me before and this time he never turned a hair.'

'Have you done for him?' she said in a whisper.

He nodded. 'The world's well rid of him. He was a mad dog.' It suddenly occurred to him that Anne Murray was in the clear now. He cursed softly. If only he had some means of letting her know.

Rose gently swabbed blood away with a sponge from the sink and said, 'It looks bad, Mr Fallon. You need a doctor and your skin's turned a funny colour along the edge of this bandage. It smells rotten.'

He got to his feet and walked over to the mirror above the fireplace and looked at his

288

chest. On the left side, below the new wound, the flesh that lined the old bandage was puffed up and angry looking. He stared at it in horror as the realization of what was happening dawned on him. He went back to the chair and sat down. 'Patch me up,' he said, 'the best way you can. Get cotton wool and a sheet. Rip it up into strips and bind me up tight.'

She produced cotton wool from a cupboard and pulled a sheet down from the airing rack that hung from the ceiling. As she worked, Fallon was thinking. He had only a few hours at the most – if he was to survive at all he needed hospital treatment badly. He laughed shortly. No wonder he had been getting the attacks of agonizing pain when poison from that first wound was steadily creeping through his entire body. He had to cross the border by evening and there was only one way of doing that – by train.

Rose was criss-crossing the bandages around his shoulder. She looped them under his armpit and around the neck in a figure of eight. When she had finished, Fallon could hardly move the arm. He managed a grin. 'That's fine,' he said. 'Now, can you get me a clean shirt and another jacket?'

She nodded. 'I think so. I'll see what I can dig up.' She was gone for several minutes. When she returned she was carrying a white, collarless shirt and a presentable grey tweed jacket. 'This is the jacket from his best suit,' she said. The shirt was the type that unbuttoned right down the front and she managed to ease it over his bandaged arm quite successfully. She buttoned it up and then produced a green silk scarf which she knotted round his neck and tucked into the shirt. When she had helped him into the jacket he regarded himself in the mirror.

'You've done a grand job,' he said.

'I'd do anything for you, Mr Fallon. You know that.' She began to feed his blood-stained shirt to the fire. 'What are we going to do now?' she said.

He sat down carefully in the chair again. 'That's the tricky bit. I've got to get out of here. Somehow, I must get on a train that's going south. But I don't want you involved in this any more than I can help. As soon as I've gone you must get in touch with the police and report this. Tell them I threatened you.'

She sighed. 'It's a bad business, but at least one good thing's come out of it. I'll be able to get away from this place.'

Fallon leaned back in his chair and knitted his brows. 'The real problem now is how the hell do I get into that station with all those police about.'

She frowned and then her face lit up and she said excitedly, 'I've got it!' She looked at the clock on the mantelpiece. 'There's a train at noon that crosses the border passing through Castlemore and Carlington. There are two packages in the van – china the old fella got at a sale. He's re-sold them to a dealer in Castlemore and they're to go by rail.'

'How does all this help me?' Fallon said.

She explained. 'I'll take you to the station in the van – I can drive it, you know. I'll get your ticket and then I'll drive in through the goods entrance to deliver the parcels.

We usually unload them at the side of the platform. You can hide inside the van. When I tell you it's all clear, you can jump out on to the platform and get straight on the train. You won't need to pass through the station hall and the ticket barrier at all.'

'But I told you I didn't want to involve you any further,' he said. 'You've got to inform the police of what has happened here as soon as I've gone.'

She shrugged. 'It'll only take me twenty minutes to take you to the station and see you safely off. What difference will twenty minutes make? I'll come straight back here and then inform them. I can tell them I fainted or something like that.'

He frowned and closed his eyes. He felt weak and his brain wouldn't work properly. He didn't want to use the girl. He knew it was wrong and yet it was a good plan and the only chance he had of getting on the train without being recognized. Once aboard he could go to sleep in a corner seat with his hat over his eyes or hide in one of the toilets. A couple of hours and he'd be in Castlemore.

He could leave the train at one of the small country stations between there and the border and cross over on foot. It could be done. There was still a chance for him. He smiled up at the girl. 'All right, I'll do it,' he said.

She smiled excitedly. 'I was worried for a minute. I thought you might refuse to let me help. It wouldn't have been fair after all you've done for me.' She went out of the room and Fallon leaned back in the chair, his face breaking into a grin. What an impossible child she was. What he had done for her, indeed!

When she returned she was wearing a coat and gloves. 'Come on!' she said. 'We haven't got much time.' He got to his feet and she helped him into his trenchcoat and belted it round his waist. He paused at the door as a thought struck him, and went back and picked up his bloodstained jacket from the hearth where she had dropped it. He extracted the Luger from its holster and slipped it into his trenchcoat pocket and then he followed her out into the yard. She opened the back of the van and he climbed inside. There was

293

a tiny glass window that looked into the cab and Fallon said, 'If the police stop us for a search and find me in the back, I'll tell them I was threatening you with the gun through that window. All right?'

She nodded. 'All right, Mr Fallon, but they won't. Never fear.' She closed the door and locked it. He heard her climb into the cab and then the engine started shakily and they moved out of the yard into the square.

He crouched in one corner of the van and leaned against the wall. He felt bad – his wound seemed to be on fire and the pain flared up into a sudden spasm of agony every few minutes leaving him sick and gasping for breath. It took them about ten minutes to reach the railway station. Once or twice the van had to slow down in heavy traffic, but they were not stopped. Finally he felt the wheels bumping over the cobbled square in front of the station and the van came to a halt. There was a quiet knock on the wall of the cab and he crouched by the little window. 'I'm going for your ticket now,' Rose said. 'Keep quiet. There are quite a few peelers about.'

He remained in that position, kneeling by the small window, but his view was restricted and he could only see the backs of several other parked vehicles. Rose was only gone for a few minutes. When she climbed back behind the wheel she sat there for a moment pretending to examine a railway timetable and spoke quietly. 'They've got two men on the main entrance and one at each ticket barrier. I'm going to drive round to the goods entrance now. The man on the gate knows me – I've been through many times. There's bound to be another peeler there so don't you be making a sound.'

'All right,' he said. 'But if anything goes wrong remember what I said – I've been holding a gun on you.'

She made no further reply and a moment later the van reversed and moved off again. He slid down to the floor and scrambled towards the rear doors. He had hardly reached them when the van slowed and halted. He held his breath and waited. Steps approached the van and he heard Rose say loudly, 'Come on, Tommy! Open up! I've got a couple of parcels for the noon train to Carlington.'

A man's voice said, 'Oh, it's you, Rose.' There was a snatch of conversation which he was unable to hear, and then another voice joined in. There was a sudden burst of laughter and Rose said, 'Oh, quit your fooling and open the gate, Tommy.' A moment later the van moved forward again and Fallon released his breath in a long sigh.

The van stopped and he heard her walk round to the rear of the vehicle. There was the unearthly shriek of a whistle and somewhere in the vicinity an engine was raising steam. Rose raised the bar that closed the doors and said quietly, 'Be ready, Mr Fallon. There are one or two porters about. When I pull these doors open jump straight out, then turn and help me pull out the parcels.'

'I'm ready whenever you are,' Fallon said. He closed his eyes as another wave of pain coursed through his body. He ground his nails into the palms of his hands and breathed slowly and deeply, and then the doors were suddenly jerked open.

He jumped to the ground, turned, and pulled one of the parcels forward. 'Has anyone noticed?' he said without raising his head.

Rose looked round casually. 'No, it seems to have worked,' she said. 'Now bring one of those parcels and follow me.'

The parcel wasn't heavy and yet the perspiration stood in beads on Fallon's brow as he followed the girl up the ramp and along the greasy platform. The train stood waiting in a gentle drift of steam. Rose went straight to the guard's van. For the moment there was no one there, and they deposited the parcels and moved back along the platform.

There were very few people on board. Fallon opened the door of an empty carriage near the rear of the train and they climbed in and stood in the corridor. 'Better keep out of sight,' he said. 'There are too few people on that platform to give me any kind of screen.'

She nodded. 'Yes, it would be a pity to get caught now.' She smiled. 'There were two of them on the goods yard gate. Luckily the porter on duty there knows me.' She shook her head and said with a grimace, 'I wouldn't like to go through it again, though, I was shaking in my shoes in case they decided to search the van.'

He smiled and squeezed her hand. 'You've been a real trooper.' She was standing on the opposite side of the narrow corridor, facing him so that their bodies were almost touching. The station was quiet. There was an air of hushed expectancy over everything. The girl's eyes, dark and luminous, were fastened on his face and suddenly tears sprang to them. He reached forward and clumsily patted her. 'Don't worry,' he said. 'I'll be all right.'

'Oh, I pray to God you will be,' she said. She stared fixedly into his face and then she took a half-pace forward into his arms and kissed him passionately. For a moment she clung there and then she tore herself free, stepped on to the platform, and closed the door.

As the whistle sounded shrilly from the end of the platform, Fallon reached for his wallet. He pulled out all that was left of the money O'Hara had given him. There was just over a hundred pounds. He extracted five one pound notes and slipped them back into the wallet; then he pushed the bundle of money into her hands. 'There, that's for you,' he said. 'There's over a hundred. Use it well. Get clear away from this place. Make a new life for yourself.'

Her eyes grew round with astonishment as she looked at the money. 'But I can't take this,' she said. 'It's too much.' The train began to move slowly and she walked along the platform keeping pace with him.

He shook his head. 'Keep it,' he said. 'It isn't any use to me now. Besides, you've earned every penny of it.'

The train was moving faster now and she started to run. Her eyes were brimming with tears. 'I'll never forget you, Mr Fallon. Not as long as I live.'

A sudden lump moved into his throat and he said unsteadily, 'I'll never forget you, Rose.' And then she was gone and the platform receded, carrying her away into the past.

He sat in the corner of an empty compartment and stared out of the window. Everything

was in the hands of fate now. A few hours
would see him at the border. Once there
he would have to take his chances, but if he
waited for darkness it shouldn't prove too
difficult to cross over on foot Another spasm
of savage pain lifted in his body. He closed
his eyes and leaned back in the corner and
after a while he drifted into a state somewhere between sleeping and waking.

About half an hour later he opened his eyes
and realized that the train had stopped. It was
standing in a tiny country station. He started
to relax again, closing his eyes, and then he
suddenly stiffened and sat forward. There was
no scheduled stop before Castlemore on this
train. He hastily pulled down the window and
glanced out. At the far end of the train, next
to the engine, a small group of men were
talking. One of them was the guard, the other
three wore the dark uniforms of the constabulary.

Fallon suddenly felt an insane desire to
laugh rise up inside him. He was losing his grip.
He should have thought of this. It was so
obviously the clever thing to do. Even as he

watched, the three policemen and the guard boarded the train and the platform started slipping away.

He moved quickly out of the compartment and along the corridor to the nearest door. As he put his hand out to open it the platform disappeared and the train moved out into the country again, gathering speed. For a moment he considered his position. He didn't have very long. There weren't many people on board and it would only take the three policemen ten or fifteen minutes to work their way through the train. He leaned out of the window and glanced along the track. There was a goods train standing on a side line a few hundred yards away. His mind worked rapidly assessing the risk, and then he smiled and opened the carriage door. There really was no risk in anything now. There was only what he had to do.

He grasped the hand rail firmly and closed the door behind him. The train was doing about twenty miles an hour and yet the stationary goods train seemed to rush towards him. He waited until it was twenty or thirty yards away and jumped.

In the split second before he landed he knew he had miscalculated the speed. His feet hit the gravel and he desperately tucked in his head as he somersaulted and crashed heavily to the ground.

For several moments he lay sprawled half-across the track upon which the goods train stood and his senses reeled. A small, insistent voice forced him to his feet and sent him lurching towards the goods train. His whole body was on fire with pain and his mind tried to take refuge from the shock of it. He reached the end waggon and reached up and pulled on the sliding door. The effort sent fresh waves of agony rippling through him. He gritted his teeth and heaved on the door and it opened. For a moment he rested there and then he pulled himself up into the waggon.

It was full of packing cases and there was little room between them. He leaned on the door with all his remaining strength and closed it. He turned and moved forward until he was standing in a small space between some packing cases and the side of the waggon.

His head was swimming and the pain was a living thing that would not leave him alone.

There was something warm and sticky trickling down inside his shirt. Almost casually he reached a hand inside his coat and took it out again. It was covered with blood. His wound had broken open. For a moment he regarded it in horror and then, as the pain rose inside him, he half-stifled a scream and crumpled to the floor.

12

He emerged from a deep well of agony and huddled on the floor in the narrow space between the packing cases and the side of the waggon, gasping for breath as the pain ebbed and flowed in his helpless body.

It was like that for a long time – a very long time. Gradually he forced the pain away from him, down to another place, below the level of his consciousness. It was there and yet it was not there. He giggled furiously and opened his eyes and found himself in darkness.

A slight feeling of panic moved inside him and he reached out through the dark and touched the side of the waggon as if to reassure himself that it was still there. The train was moving very slowly along the track and nearby he could hear the sound of other trains.

He felt light-headed and he searched his pockets until he found a packet of cigarettes. He pushed one into his mouth and his fingers fumbled for a match. It flared in his cupped hands and he leaned forward to light the cigarette and stayed in that position, the match burning in his right hand.

The floor around him was covered with blood. It had seeped through his jacket. The left sleeve and side of his trenchcoat were saturated in it. The match flame reached his fingers and he dropped it and sat staring into the darkness. His mind was crystal clear and he felt curiously calm. He braced his hands between the packing cases and the wall and pushed himself upright.

He started to move, walking slowly and carefully, feeling his way with outstretched hands. His fingers scraped against the sliding door and they gripped the edge of it and pulled hard. A sudden drift of rain was blown through the door into his face. He held on tight to the handrail and leaned in the opening staring out.

It was dark outside and raining quite hard. The train was passing through a maze of tracks and some distance away he could see a lighted platform. A moment later they rumbled past a signal box and he glanced up quickly to see the name of the station. It was Castlemore. Underneath the sign there was a large, illuminated electric clock. The hands pointed to half-past six. He lit the cigarette and slid down to the floor and considered the position.

The train he had boarded at Stramore had left at noon. He had jumped from it perhaps half an hour later. That meant he had been lying unconscious for something like six hours with his life's blood draining out of his body. Panic moved in him and he pulled himself up in the doorway and stood erect. A man couldn't bleed for six hours – there wasn't that much blood in him.

He slipped a hand inside his jacket and gently probed the wound. The bleeding seemed to have stopped. He tried to think calmly. Obviously the wound had been wrenched open by his clumsy fall from the train. He must have bled for a while and then the blood had clotted. After all, the bandage was still in position. He laughed shakily. There was no need to worry. No need for panic. He was still on his feet. There was a chance yet.

He sat down on the floor again and looked out at the lights of Castlemore as they receded into the darkness. The next stop was Carlington. All he had to do was sit tight. He could leave the train outside Carlington and reach the border on foot. He could be home by morning.

The train travelled along at ten or fifteen miles an hour, and he looked back at the lights and lapsed into a reverie. He remembered that first morning when he had walked through the town in the rain and Murphy had followed him. He could see the boy now, bareheaded in the timber yard, brushing the mud from his cap and cursing. Poor Johnny Murphy – looking for the high adventure and all he had found was death.

And then there was Anne – lovely Anne Murray. It had taken him a while to realize that she was beautiful or perhaps he'd known it all along. Perhaps he simply hadn't wanted to admit it. He stared into the darkness and for a moment her face seemed to materialize out of the night. Her eyes were deep pools and he was drowning in the depths of them. He laughed high pitched and unearthly. There was no hope for him there – no hope at all. To receive it was first necessary to give and he had given her nothing – nothing at all.

He laughed bitterly. It was almost funny. Everything he touched he destroyed. Murphy, Rogan, and Anne Murray – perhaps her most of all he had destroyed. There was only one thing he wasn't sorry about. He'd come over the border to save a man and had ended up by killing him, but he wasn't sorry. He wasn't sorry at all. There were some men who were not fit to live and Patrick Rogan had been one of them.

He frowned and his wandering mind tried to grapple with the problem of how you told a woman you have promised to help, that you had failed her. How was he to stand before Maureen Rogan and tell her that he had killed her son? How was he to make her understand? He sighed and leaned back against one of the packing cases and then the train shuddered and began to skid to a halt as the brakes were applied.

There was a sudden silence that was broken only by the hiss of steam and then he heard voices coming along the track. He got to his feet and peered outside. There were lanterns moving towards him through the darkness. They halted and there was the sound of a door being opened. After a few moments the lanterns moved down to the next waggon and he heard another door being opened.

Fallon didn't hesitate. Almost without thinking, he dropped to the ground and moved across the track. For a moment he stood poised on the edge of the embankment, straining his eyes into the darkness, and then he took a step forward and lost his balance. He rolled over and over down the bank, crashing through a plantation of young fir trees, the branches whipping his sides. The darkness became a whirling mass of coloured lights and the pain enveloped him. That terrible pain that started somewhere in his chest and flooded throughout his entire body, gripping his lungs in a paralysis so that he had to struggle for breath.

He came to rest against a larger tree and lay there for several minutes until his breathing was easier. When he got to his feet he stood swaying in the darkness, reaching out his hands before him as if looking for something to hang on to.

He started to blunder down through the plantation, the branches slashing across his face and a terrible panic moved in him and he began to run, staggering through the trees with his head bent and his right arm held up as a shield. He fell several times but each time scrambled to his feet and ran faster, as if something terrible and nameless was at his heels.

He crashed out of the plantation, caught his foot in a tussock of grass, and went sprawling down a short slope into a ditch. He clawed his way out of a foot of muddy water, soaked to the skin, and found himself on the main road. He started to run at a jog trot into the darkness, the rain lashing against his face. He didn't know why he was running – it was simply that he had a long way to go and so very little time – so very little time.

Through the trees ahead of him he noticed a red glow staining the sky and he began to laugh foolishly. Perhaps it was hell that was waiting for him there in the darkness. He turned the bend in the road and halted. Some fifty yards along on the right hand side of the road there was a roadhouse and a great, red neon sign sizzled in the rain. For a moment he stood there, swaying, and then he stumbled forward towards it.

He crouched down in the shelter of a low wall and peered over the top. The sound of music drifted from an open window and now and then a snatch of careless laughter. There was a car park over the wall and he moved cautiously towards the entrance. There seemed to be no one about. He moved quickly inside and ran from vehicle to vehicle trying the doors desperately. Within a few moments he had found an old van that was unlocked. He wrenched open the door and his hand probed across the dash-board. The keys were hanging where the owner had left them.

He put a foot on the running board and a hand grabbed him by the shoulder and a voice said, 'Now then – what the hell do you think you're doing?'

He didn't bother to reply – he had no time for words. His hand jerked the Luger from his pocket and he turned and wiped it across the white face, dimly seen through the darkness. The man sank to the ground with a low groan and Fallon scrambled into the cab, pressed the starter, and reversed out of the car park. Within a few moments he was rushing through the darkness, the headlights slicing a path before him.

His lights picked out a white sign-post when he was still some little way from it and he braked hard and leaned out of the window to read the sign.

He was on the right road. Carlington was fifteen miles away. He moved into gear and drove away. The most the van would do was fifty and he pressed his foot flat on the boards and lay back in the seat, his hands steady on the wheel, his eyes peering into the darkness.

The night was playing tricks on him. At one moment it seemed dark and then it would lighten in some curious way. He screwed his eyes up tightly several times and shook his head. Perhaps it was the headlights. Only the headlights. And then it happened again, but this time, the light grew and grew until he seemed to see the whole countryside spread on either side of him. It was as if he was flying above it looking down and that wasn't right. That couldn't be right. He screamed and slammed his foot hard against the brake and the van slewed to a halt, drifting at an angle along the road.

He leaned against the wheel, his head down, and cried bitterly, the sobs tearing his whole body. I don't want to die, he told himself. I mustn't die. I must get home. I must get home. Suddenly he realized why it was so important. Anne was waiting for him. She was waiting there at his cottage across the border from Doone. She was waiting for him and he couldn't let her down.

It was almost with a sense of surprise that he found himself driving forward into the darkness again. His hands were steady on the wheel and one small, firm corner of his mind was concentrating with all its power on keeping them there. The van lifted over a slight hill and down below him in a hollow he saw the lights of a small village. He passed along the village street, empty and forlorn in the rain, and ahead of him, on the right-hand side, he saw a round white bowl of light shining through the dark.

He stopped the van and scrambled out. The round lamp was perched on top of a tall, brick gate and etched on it in black letters was the name, Patrick Quinn, M.D. Fallon opened the gate and walked towards the front door.

The path went on for ever and the door seemed to be receding from him. Suddenly it loomed over him and then it turned completely on to its side. It took him several moments to realize that his cheek was pillowed on the ground. Slowly and wearily he scrambled to his feet and fell against the door. He raised his fist and hammered weakly against it. It opened so suddenly that he fell in and then strong arms picked him up and a door opened and a hall stretched before him.

He was lying on a couch and there was a confused babble of voices and then a face was looking down at him – a narrow face, topped by white hair. A face full of sympathy and understanding. Fallon moistened his lips and tried to speak, 'Lost blood,' he croaked. 'Lot of blood – been bleeding for hours. Help me. I mustn't die.' He half-raised himself. 'I mustn't die!'

A hand gently pushed him back and a quiet voice, the voice of one who had lived long and seen most things, said, 'I'll help you, son. Just take it easy and lie still.'

Hands lifted him upright and carefully stripped his coat and jacket from him and he was laid back against the pillow again. Something moved along his chest and he looked down and saw a pair of scissors neatly parting his shirt and the bandages underneath. There was a sudden, terrified gasp of horror and a woman's voice said, 'Oh, my God!'

He struggled up on one elbow and saw a young woman standing at one side of the couch holding a basin and then the scissors completed their work and the bandages were cut away. Immediately a dreadful smell became apparent. Fallon heard the old man say quickly, 'Bandages – hurry. There's no time to lose.'

Again he was lifted upright and he felt bandages encircle his body again. He was perfectly conscious of all that was taking place and yet it was as if he was an outsider looking in on all this – as if it were happening to someone else in another time – another place. The room began to undulate and the ceiling heaved. He was laid gently back against the pillow and closed his eyes. He was going to make it. He was going back to his cottage and Anne would be waiting. She would be waiting and nothing was going to stop him from getting there. Then why was he lying here?

The thought came as a complete surprise. A few miles away was the border and he was lying here. He opened his eyes and saw that a needle was fixed in his arm by a piece of sticking plaster and from the needle a tube ran to a bottle which was held above his head by the woman. 'What am I doing here?' he said. He pushed himself into a sitting position pulling on the tube so that she had to step forward quickly. 'What am I doing here?' he demanded again.

The woman's eyes were round with fear and there were tears in them. 'Please lie down,' she said. 'You must lie down.'

There was a moment of silence and through it he could hear the voice of the old man saying, 'Yes – he's here now. No – he's not dangerous, you fool. Yes, I'm sure it's Martin Fallon.' There was a pause and the voice went on, 'An ambulance as quickly as you can and if you can't get one here within half an hour, you'd better send a hearse – he's dying.'

Through the terrible soundless quiet that followed, Fallon shook his head awkwardly from side to side and great, heavy tears coursed slowly from his eyes. 'No,' he said. 'I'm not dying – I won't die. I'm going home.'

He stood up and wrenched his arm away and the needle tore his flesh sending a bright spurt of red blood running over the white skin. His bloody jacket was on the floor and he dropped to one knee and fumbled in the pockets until his hand closed over the butt of the Luger. He came erect as the doctor burst into the room. The old man barred the door, arms outstretched and Fallon said, 'Out of the way. I'm not dying. Got an appointment to keep. Got to meet Anne.'

'You're sick,' the old man said. 'You've got to lie down.'

Fallon pointed the Luger straight at him. 'Move!' he said harshly. 'I'm going to Doone if it kills me.'

The old man shook his head. 'You won't even get to the door,' he said. For a moment he looked directly into Fallon's face and then an expression of great compassion showed in his eyes and he stood to one side. Fallon staggered out into the hall, wrenched open the front door, and lurched down the path.

The van started at once. He moved rapidly away from the white light, away into the darkness and the rain on his last journey. His mind seemed to clear for a while and he began to think coherently again. He noticed that he was still holding the Luger in his right hand. It was awkward and hindered him from handling the wheel properly. With a casual, unthinking gesture he threw it out of the window into the night. The upper part of his body was naked except for the bandages and yet he felt no cold and was conscious of no discomfort. He was going home and Anne would be waiting for him – that was all that mattered.

The rain increased into a heavy downpour that flooded across the windscreen so that he could hardly see ahead of him. It didn't matter. Nothing mattered. There was nothing to fear any more. He was going home and nothing could stop him – he had to keep his appointment.

A house appeared on the right and then another and another. He topped a rise and went down a short hill that was lined on each side with houses and he knew he was at Doone. He swung the wheel sharply at the bottom of the hill and turned into a long, tree-lined avenue and there at the end, under the floodlight, was the border post.

He felt no fear because there was nothing to be afraid of. He was going through and nothing could stop him. No one would hinder him. They would know. There was a man in a heavy raincoat standing under the light in the porch out of the rain. Fallon halted the van and waited.

His mind was no longer a part of his body. It ranged high in the rain, looking down on the small border post and the men within it. The man in the blue raincoat started towards him from the porch and then a voice called. A tall figure emerged from the interior of the hut. He stood, erect and handsome in his uniform with raincoat thrown carelessly over his shoulders, and held a rapid conversation with the Customs' man. The other went into the hut and the tall man stepped down into the rain and came towards the van.

When he was a few paces away he recoiled

suddenly and a startled gasp came from his mouth. Fallon smiled and said, 'Hello, Phil. Fancy meeting you here.'

Stuart moved forward and leaned in at the window. There was utter horror in his face. 'Martin!' he cried. 'For God's sake, Martin!'

Fallon glanced down. There was blood coursing over his chest. He looked vacantly at Stuart and said, 'I'm going home, Phil. I'm going home. Don't try to delay me, old man. I haven't much time.'

For a moment Philip Stuart stared helplessly at him and then a peculiar expression appeared on his face. Walking slowly like a man in a dream, he moved to the bar that stretched across the road and raised it.

Fallon drove straight through without looking back. He felt strong and powerful again. He had done it. He was back across the border and he was going home. The road dipped and he splashed through a ford and swerved into a side road on the other side.

Below him was the valley and down there beneath the mountain a solitary light gleamed. He pressed his foot against the boards and the car flew through the night like some great bird returning home. He braked hard at the bottom of the hill, his wheels skidding in loose gravel and turned into the final road for home. The gateposts jumped out of the darkness to meet him. He braked again and swung the wheel but his hands had lost their strength. The van lifted on two wheels, spun in a half-circle and crashed against a gatepost.

The door opened to his touch and he fell out on to the ground. For a moment he lay there and then he scrambled wearily to his feet and began to walk towards the cottage. The light in the window seemed to grow brighter and there was a sound of voices. The door was flung open and a long shaft of light picked him out of the darkness. There was a sudden silence.

Fallon stood there, swaying slightly, his feet braced apart. He was aware of the coldness of the rain as it fell on his bare skin and somehow, he had lost a shoe and a stone was cutting into his foot. His eyes were dazzled by the light so that he had difficulty in seeing properly. He recognized O'Hara and Doolan was standing at his shoulder and then they were pushed aside and she was there. For one long moment he looked at her and tried to smile and then he took a single, hesitant pace towards her and fell forward.

He opened his eyes and saw O'Hara bending over him. 'We'll avenge you, Martin,' he said. 'We'll not forget.'

Fallon began to laugh. It all seemed so stupid and meaningless now – words, just words. And then O'Hara was pushed aside and Anne was kneeling in the rain and he was in her arms. He tried to speak but the words wouldn't come. He wanted to tell her that he loved her, that she was the thing that had been missing in his life.

It was no use. She was crying and he wanted to comfort her but he felt very weak. It had all been such a damned waste – his whole life had been wasted.

She was crying steadily now, her arms tightly wrapped around him. He smiled contentedly and turned his face towards the warmth and then it was cold – very cold and everything was slipping away from him. It felt as if a great wind was trying to lift him up and carry him away to the other end of time. For a little while longer he clung to her and then he let go and turned his face towards the darkness.

What's next?

Tell us the name of an author you love

| Jack Higgins | Go ► |

and we'll find your next great book.